Michelene Esposito

Spinsters Ink
2007

Spinsters Ink
P.O. Box 242
Midway, Florida 32343

Printed in the United States of America on acid-free paper
First Edition

Editor: Christi Cassidy
Cover designer: KIARO Creative Ltd.

ISBN10: 1-883523-85-0
ISBN 13: 978-1-883523-85-5

For Diana

Acknowledgments

If your words and thoughts see the light of day and, better yet, the printed page, you are lucky indeed. I am so grateful to those who helped me along the way as *Mermaid* and I made our journey.

Thank you, as always, to Diana Moore, my first editor and best friend, for the early reading and revision recommendations to the manuscript. Thanks for always letting me pick up the phone and knock around this character development, that plot twist, whenever I've needed to. And, even more so, thank you for your friendship and support, love and shared laughter all these many years.

And thank you to my son, Benjamin. My love for you and the extraordinary joy of motherhood has fueled much creativity and helped me to grow as a person and writer. You are my greatest gift and I thank the gods and goddesses each day for the privilege of being your mother.

Sara Joyce and Linda Hill at Spinsters have been wonderful and professional in all our work together and I am grateful to them for bringing *Mermaid* to print.

I am honored to have Nancy Ellis as my agent—warm, knowledgeable, funny and accessible. I'm so happy to have you on my team!

Christi Cassidy is the reason you can even read this novel. Her edits were vital to producing the final manuscript and if you add her compassion and humor to her skill you have a powerful package indeed. I am humbled by her knowledge.

Vivian Hudson shared her experience in the Sisterhood with me and helped me to shape Liza's experience. Michael D'Orazi of the Alameda Fire Department helped me to understand the training and life of a firefighter. Thank you for so generously sharing your experiences.

And thank you to Lorrie Goldin for helping me find my way. Your rye humor and spot-on insights have woven their way into my person and into this story.

And for my husband, Rafael, who came home one day to find his new wife missing in action as she buried herself in an office, obsessed with final edits—I am grateful for your loving support and your interest in my work.

As always, thank you to my parents, Eleanor and Michael. You are the reason I know how to love, how to write about love—and how deeply one *can* love.

Chapter 1

It was icy cold. The red seats of the car felt clammy and I traced a scratch in the leather with my fingertip. My mother wouldn't turn off the engine. It kept humming, gunning suddenly with a little lurch that made Kate and me clutch across the seat for each other's hands. I was seven at the time, small for my age, and I couldn't see over the seat. All I could see was a dull gray sky waiting to burst, growing darker each minute we stayed parked on that dock. I rooted around in my pockets but only found one glove and set to work squeezing both hands into the glove.

She had said, "Go get some hot cocoa from that truck," but Kate had said no, it was okay, and she was the oldest and knew better.

I knew it was bad. You don't turn down a hot cocoa on a cold day. A couple frozen raindrops slapped the window and melted down. The windows started growing fog except where the defroster blew a clearing on the windshield. And the engine kept running.

"Girls," she said, clicking open her purse, taking out a cigarette and a lighter, pausing to light it and inhale and exhale, "there are days, dark days like today, but the nights are worse, too dark to find your way." Kate pinched my palm hard with her nail.

Those are the two things I remember right. Two chances. The coffee truck was at the end of the dock by the street. Three or four hard-hatted men gathered around the truck drinking coffee, dunking doughnuts they ate in three bites. We could have gotten out and then run to the truck for help. "Dark days" meant things were about to go very bad. It was always that way. A wind, so strong it howled, hit the car and we rocked in a way that made me gasp. Then there was a clanking sound that I couldn't place, felt too frozen scared to scoot up and peer over the back of the front seat. A click I couldn't place either. The car gave a rock backward and started rolling forward and we knew. We screamed. Whenever I remember this I think I heard my mother scream too but Kate swears she didn't make a sound. I could see Kate's face, her mouth open so wide I could see inside, holding the same note, until we hit the water, rocking side to side. It was then that I realized the seats felt clammy because the front passenger window was open, saltwater smells, green water rising above the windows. Then there was nothing but green and I thought, *I'll be a mermaid.* A piece of seaweed passed by, winding in the murky water, the water rushing, falling in the open window, sliding down the door, puddling at my feet and I thought, *I'll grow a tail, green and scaly.*

Kate tells me she was pushing me the whole time and that I was wrong. It was the window on my mother's side that was open—and not a crack, all the way open. She swears I was so good, did just what she said and grabbed onto the window and the side of the door, pushing myself into the bay, that she came right out after me, couldn't see me for a second and panicked. We floated up fast and by then the men were there. I aimed for a pair of black boots. The man who scooped me out of the water swam with one arm circling my body, pulling me along with his kicks and strokes to the dock where another man pulled me out of the water and threw a pea-green snorkel coat over me, the weight of it sinking me to a kneel on the dock. And as I knelt there, my world a swirl of denim legs running and shouts, I looked up to see a little boy watching me from the back window of a blue pickup. He looked so frightened. I watched him, watched over him, like something of my own, until they slammed the ambulance door and we pulled away.

It was January and the water was close to freezing. Even if they could have gone back down for my mother it was chains I had heard and the kind of lock with a combination Kate used for gym at the middle school. They found the combination in her purse; typed numbers on a slip of paper the size of a cookie fortune. I think that means she wasn't so sure she wanted to do it. Kate thinks she did it to taunt us with how easy it would have been to save her if we'd been smart enough to look in her purse.

We were at San Francisco General by the time they pulled the car up out of the bay.

I've had these dreams since then that my mother is a mermaid. The dreams were so real after she died I would beg to go to the beach. I knew better than to tell my grandparents I wanted to visit my mother, and I knew if I said that, Kate wouldn't go with me. She hated my mother for what she'd done and even by the summer I was too afraid to go in the water without Kate, because sometimes in the dreams my mother would reach out, her beautiful hair a floating dance in front of her face, and grab my ankle, pull me down.

We were in the papers, on the news. Sometimes I think they transferred us from San Francisco General to Oakland Children's Hospital for that week just to keep us away from it all, because physically we were fine. A psychiatric resident—a tiny woman in a too-big white coat with a nervousness that threatened to push through the line where her jagged, bitten nails met the pink membrane of fingertips—sat on the floor in the day room with us each day asking if we wanted to talk about it. Kate did most of the talking, tried to explain to this woman that our beautiful mother was frail as a twig, arms and legs so long and delicate anyone could see she was breakable. I tried to get a word in edgewise and said, "She missed Daddy," but Kate shot me a look like I'd betrayed some secret. I shot the look right back at her. A secret's not a secret unless you tell the person so. Everyone knew she missed him. True, all fathers went to work but the day is long when you have a love like my mother had for my father.

Maybe if they'd let us go to the funeral for one last look her long legs would have etched their place in our Jell-O-y minds and I wouldn't have had the mermaid dreams. But Kate says she's glad she didn't go, that she was so sad she would have spread open the lid from the box and landed, a topple of relief, right inside the coffin with my mother.

I remember playing Go Fish on the linoleum floor of the unit hall and not a bit of Kate being sad. They gave us pink Benedryls to help us sleep. One night I woke up and Kate wasn't in the bed. I flew out of the room and into the bright hall light. She was sitting in a nurse's lap with a half-sized can of apple juice and a straw. She was eleven and way too old for laps. I asked for a can, too. Kate says I stuck to her like the sick-sweet smelling bubblegum on the blacktop of parking lots. "So?" I reply. "What did you expect?" That shuts her up.

Chapter 2

My grandparents' house felt strangely foreign the day we left the hospital. I clutched the coloring book one of the nurses, Faye, gave me as a good-bye gift. She'd cried silent dripping tears when we left.

"Sit yourself right down there, May," my grandmother said, pointing to the little mat in front of the door, "and take your shoes off."

Kate got to take hers off, clutching the wall just in time, just before my grandfather roared, "Get your hands off the wall before I hand you a paintbrush!"

We tucked our chins, eyes meeting, lips with a hint of a smile. Our grandfather had been yelling at us to get our hands off the walls and turn off the lights our whole lives. Sometimes the best medicine is the familiar, whatever shape it takes.

He was tall, with the soft, slack face of age and large, rough hands from working the farm they used to own in Pennsylvania. He took a walk each morning with Trish, their poodle, around the neighborhood and picked pieces of trash up off the ground. He had a little plastic produce bag he kept in his windbreaker pocket specifically for that purpose.

I started out after the two of them one morning. The first time I didn't really want to be with them and I lagged a good half-block behind, kicking this little slate stone down the sidewalk. We made it all the way back to the house without a word to each other and had he not paused, holding the screen door ajar for me to step under his arm, I would have thought he hadn't seen me. Eventually, he'd call for me when it was time to go and I started picking up my own pieces of trash. My grandmother scolded us about picking up filthy garbage, catching Hepatitis B and God Knows What Else. My grandfather said the same thing over and over, "What are we doing here, Em? We're washing our hands. We always wash our hands—straight from the backdoor to the sink. I'm not seeing the problem with this if we wash our hands," and I'd listen to them argue, going back and forth, like the warm water and the slippery soap.

I don't recall us saying much of anything on those walks, just my grandfather muttering to himself, "Freaking pigs," or, "A *sin*," as he bent over for a piece of trash. We didn't talk about anything, let alone my mother's suicide, her attempt to kill us and my feelings about all of that. I asked him years later, out of the blue, over a paper plate of barbecued hotdogs and macaroni salad, why he took me on those walks.

"You seemed to take to it and I figured fresh air was probably just the thing."

He kept fruit trees—fig, apricot, peach—lining the back fence. I'd whine at him till he'd pull a peach from the tree so the branch sprang back and then cut me wedge after wedge with a red pocketknife that hung from his key chain. We'd let the juice run down our chins, sticky and warm from the sun.

Then he'd hand me the pit and I'd run off to plant it with him yelling after me, "Watch where you plant that thing. I don't need a damned orchard in the front yard."

My grandparents had moved to Alameda from Pennsylvania after I was born. They had that house built special, big cement blocks, stone fireplace, heavy doors and extra beams.

"This place is built like a brick shithouse," my grandfather liked to say.

Our house was three doors down, a three-bedroom gingerbread Victorian in yellow with white trim.

My father was tall, taller than his own father, six feet, six inches, tall enough for my mother to order a special bed for their room and a special couch for the living room. His name was Henry, which I always thought was too short and skinny of a name.

I don't want to even tell you how many therapists I've had in my life between my mother trying to drown us and then all of Kate's drama, but it probably was the only thing that kept me afloat. In the eighth grade one of them, Dr. Eliot, a young woman with a thick rope of blond hair down to her rear, told me that it would have been better for my father and grandparents to take me back to my own house. People do the best they can and she wasn't judging them or blaming them, just stating a fact. As it was, my father was there by himself and we'd go by every few days those first months to pick something up, more underwear, Colorforms, Kate's diary, and then back again for the little gold key she kept hanging from pink embroidery string from a nail on the inside wall of her closet. I knew she was forgetting the key but I wasn't supposed to know where it was in the first place, so I started to say something and then shut my mouth.

It's funny how quickly, easily really, people fall into a routine. I think human beings must crave routine, however dismal, because then you know at least what will happen next. You don't have to worry about something jumping out and scaring you. When I first caught Kate carving away at her thigh with a paperclip she told me in the most unbelievably calm voice that it didn't hurt, that she liked it because it was something she could count on, a tiny secret comfort flowing from an inch-long line of skin. I could see that. Even at eight.

My grandmother would make us all dinner and my father came straight from work, watched TV with us and left later after Kate and I had gone to bed. Kate asked once why the hell we couldn't just go home, but the focus ended up being on the fact that she used the word "hell" and I don't think we actually got an answer. I figure the answer was pretty simple. It was easier for my grandmother to do everything from her own house than from ours, and no one told her it was better for us to be in *our* own house, so things didn't happen—like Kate and I making up scary stories of my mother's ghost waiting to leap out from our grandparents' swimming pool. She would have done whatever she was told was best for us. It's just that no one knew what that was at the time.

Kate thinks the reason we stayed at my grandparents' was so that my father could have his girlfriend—the real reason my mother drove off the dock—to the house whenever he wanted. I never saw any proof of that. We searched the house from top to bottom, when we finally moved back that summer, for an earring or the smell of strange perfume or love notes in the back of his sock drawer. We found nothing. Kate says that's because he was so wracked by guilt by then he broke up with her and threw everything out. You can't tell her otherwise.

It took me till a couple of years ago—I'm in my thirties now—to actually *see* my father, such a dim light in comparison to my beam of a mother, and, more so, to think to ask him who he really was. It's the simplest thing to do but I'm not the only one who forgets to give it a try. I watch him with Kate. My grandfather used to say when he was alive and Kate would mouth off to my father, "What that kid needs is a good smack," and my father would still go off after her and I'd hear them in the next room making up.

There aren't many stories my father will tell about my mother. But one night, a few years ago, Kate was in the hospital following an overdose of whatever pill she was taking at the time. We got home late and sat at the kitchen table eating cookies and milk, just us, my stepmother, Betsy, having gone up to bed. And he started quietly, slowly, to tell me that when they brought me back from the hospital my mother was a dervish of anxiety, telling my father in a hushed, pressured voice, so as not to wake the baby, that she was afraid she would drop me and break one of my little shots of arm or leg, never mind the soft skull.

"You have to take her away from me. I'm afraid I'll kill her," she told him.

That's when his parents, my grandparents, moved out to California to help take care of us.

"Did you try to get her some help?" I asked carefully, not wanting to pick at the sore of guilt.

"I tried to help her, talk to her, bring her presents, make her laugh. You don't remember, May, there were plenty of times she was just fine. It wasn't a constant thing, but I just don't think they were ever able to get her medication right once we were in California. And when she was pregnant with you they wanted her off the Lithium, but that was a disaster so they put her back on and then . . ." He trailed off, shaking his head.

"What?" I asked, starving for any cracker crumb of my mother he was willing to feed me.

"Oh, May, we were so young, and I was still going to Berkeley and working and I just don't think the doctors knew what to do for her. Maybe there wasn't anything else they could have done, but nothing seemed to work—at least not for very long. And it just pains me so to see Kate this way, to see your mother's frightened eyes in her. I keep hoping all of this will help, the therapy, the medication. And I always hope, everytime there's a calm, I have to hope that all we've done has finally helped. I have to hope that's true. Otherwise I suppose I'm just waiting for her to die too."

He's right about that. What I remember of my mother is her making us English muffin pizzas, telling Kate that if she didn't stop instigating things she was going to her room. And each time I told myself that it was okay now. But it never was for long. When my mother did her "dark days" talk we played outside. Back then Kate kept an eye on me.

I feel sorry for my father. There was a time when I was obsessed with the thought that my mother had left a note. I kept nagging him about it until he told me that what she had done was called him on the phone. "She said, 'I love you, but I can't take this,' and I said, 'Liza, don't do this. Let me help you,' and she said, 'I want that more than you know,' but then she hung up. I raced home but, of course, it was hopeless. I was twenty minutes away. I should have called the police. I can't tell you how sorry I am I didn't call the police. I just was so panicked I didn't think."

I've tried to tell him that she had us in our coats, standing by the door, the car warming up, when she called him, and I don't think the police would have known where to look—over the bridge to San Francisco. And then they'd still have had to find which pier. It doesn't do any good.

He nods and says things like, "Thank you. I hear that."

And then lets Kate call him a "fucking cannibal" because she's decided to not eat meat.

Once, and only once, he turned to me, after she'd let one lose on him and stormed out of the room, and said, "That child is the devil sent to torture me to my grave."

I'm sure he probably raked himself over the coals for that one but good. I think he should get angry like that a little more often but I don't think he was right about Kate being the devil. I think, in a weird kind of way, Kate's got my mother's angel in her come to prove to my father that you really can't save a person, tear the guilt from him once and for all. I think sometimes an angel has to look like a devil to get certain jobs done.

She was in the hospital again just last month. She took a handful of Tylenol and slug after slug of some cheap whiskey that she had contracted with her therapist not to have in the house in the first place. I'm not even going to get into it with her about that. I'm not even gonna go there. The whole time we were growing up, after my mother killed herself, I lurked around my own house like some stalker keeping my eye on Kate.

My grandparents died, one after the other, when I was twelve and Kate was fifteen, and my aunts, my father's sisters, Lily and Mary Beth, flew out each time for the funeral. It was when we were sitting at the funeral home, at the viewing for my grandmother, when Aunt Lily said, "I know we haven't been around for you girls as much as we'd like to have been, but now that both Mother and Father are gone I want you both to know that we are here for you and we will be checking on you from Denver, making sure that everything is going okay. And if you ever need anything you just call us and we'll be there."

Kate looked at my aunt, her hip cocked to one side, her lipstick smeared, and told her, "The hell you will," and walked out of the funeral home.

"That's Liza's girl all right," Aunt Mary Beth said to no one in particular and she was smiling, like my sister being a nasty, reeling death wish was something we should look upon fondly.

Over the years, I've looked at enough photos of my mom to not forget what she looks like, and Kate looks too much like her—the long legs and hair, eyes that snap and gleam like a fire. My grandmother told me once, "That Liza had too much energy for being such a long drink of water, wore herself out."

I'm the shortest one in the family at five-foot-six, my hair is as straight as a stick and I'm the only one with blue eyes. It would worry me, especially as I got older, the difference, how Kate looked so much like our mother and I didn't look like anyone. I asked Henry one day while we were out raking leaves—something he seemed to do a lot after my grandparents died, to the point where he kind of ran out of leaves—if maybe I'd been adopted.

"What?" he said sharply, stopping mid-rake.

"I was just wondering. I mean, I don't understand why I don't look like anyone."

"You look like yourself," but I guess he could see I was not going to let this go. He sighed, sort of leaning on his rake, and said, "You look like your mother's mother."

"Really?"

"Yes. She was a little shorter and had straight hair and blue eyes. It was your mother's father who was tall."

There was one picture in the whole house of my mother's parents and after that I went straight to the living room and dug around in the old photo albums until I found it. It was a picture of my mother with her parents standing on either side of them. My mother is little in it and all three of them are dressed up fancy like they were going to a wedding or something.

Any time Kate and I would look through the photo albums and come across this picture we'd always ask who they were so we could hear my father say, "Those are your other grandparents." It may seem weird but we just liked to hear it, to know that there were some other people out there who were connected to us even though we never saw them.

Of course it was Kate, one day, who asked the next question, "Why don't we ever see them?"

Henry got the look he got when one of us backed him into a place he didn't want to go. He fumbled a bit and finally it was Betsy who said, "Henry, they are big girls now."

"It's complicated, Kate. They lived in Los Angeles. They came to your mother's funeral but I haven't heard from them or seen them since then. Your mother was not very close with them. It has nothing to do with you girls."

"Yeah, well, fuck them then," Kate said, slamming the photo album shut.

"Kate, we don't need that kind of language," Henry said, tensing for a battle.

"Whatever." And she just got up and walked away. None of us said anything about it after that but I knew what Kate meant—two more people who didn't want us. It was the kind of thing we both couldn't help but keep track of—grandparents who were never interested in meeting us.

Then when Kate was twenty-one the letter from the John Stewart Company came—about the trust money. No call, no card, just a lot of money, more than either of us had seen, in trust from my mother's parents for each of us when we turned twenty-one, twenty-five and thirty.

I came home from school to find Kate sitting on her bed, holding the letter, and when she told me all I could say was, "What are you going to do with all that?"

"Whatever the hell I want."

And she did. She blew it. There wasn't anything anyone could do about it either. Henry tried to reason with her but it was Betsy who said, "This is her lesson to learn. If you keep treating her like a child she'll stay a child." For whatever that was worth. It was more than she could spend anyway. She got halfway through it and then decided to put the other ten thousand in the bank.

That's pretty much the last time anyone talked about them. I looked them up years later when I was doing an Internet research project for school and I found them—their obituaries in the *Los Angeles Times*. My grandmother died when I was nineteen and my grandfather had died two years earlier. They did not mention my mother. When I came home from school and told Kate she just shrugged. She had just fired her therapist for not taking her call the night before and was hardly even listening to me as she scribbled furiously in her diary.

Kate's fired about twenty therapists but somehow keeps the same psychiatrist, Dr. Medley, an old guy who wears tortoiseshell glasses and bow ties in a stylish but somehow unaffected kind of way. I like him because he's so unflappable. During our sessions, I'd seen Kate light into him, like a spit in the face, and he'd calmly look around for the most comfortable chair in the room, sit down and wait it out. She'd call him sometimes, in the middle of the night, when she couldn't get her regular therapist on the phone, and I could almost see him get out of bed and ease himself into an armchair in the corner of his living room until she wound herself down to a damp heap of nightgown, curled up against the wall. She'd wipe her eyes and nose on the tail of the nightgown and say, "Ah-ha, yeah, okay. Two? Okay," then hang up, pulling herself off the floor saying, really to remind herself, not because she had the consideration to fill me in, "He said to take two Klonopins and call him tomorrow if it's not better."

I've done my reading up on mental illness, being a librarian, and I know it's a genetic or environmental thing, and given we had both I guess it was inevitable one of us would follow in my mother's footsteps.

I was moving out the next week. I had my own therapist, Laura, and she and I have been working up to this for close to a year. I am one pathetic coward, if you want to know the truth, and it took me that long to guts it up to do this. I did my whole B.A. and master's living at home, and while I saved enough of my trust money for the down payment on this townhouse on the Bay Farm Island part of Alameda, it was almost beside the point. I stayed because I was afraid. I'm still afraid.

The day I told Kate she smiled, real and honest, and said, "That sounds so great. I'm going to do that, too. Really, May, I'll help you paint or pack, whatever."

Kate's a fabulous seamstress. She had a job in the Southshore shopping center at a fabric store called Yards and Buttons, where she cut people's fabric and rang them up. She wanted to teach one of their sewing classes, the one on making curtains in particular, but the owner, who was pretty tolerant if you ask me, said Kate wasn't reliable enough for a ten-week class.

I went down there after my closing on the house and Kate treated me to curtains. We measured every window in the place and I picked out the fabric I wanted. A couple times I turned to her to ask what she thought of a pattern and all she'd say was, "It's your place. It has to be your choice," which I really appreciated for the love it is. Kate is someone who always has an opinion.

She made them all, a constant drone of the sewing machine and Bruce Springsteen pulsing from her room, in one weekend. She's a whiz at getting those shiny gold rods up straight with those microscopic nails they give you for the braces. We walked from room to empty room, admiring the way the drapes waved at us in the breeze, the way the yellow-and-white-checked kitchen curtains made us think of lemon meringue pie and summer. She'd embroidered the tiniest pink flowers with green stems on the edge of my bathroom curtains and I kept reaching out to finger the French knots till she knocked my hand.

"Don't get them dirty!" Then she went home and took the Tylenol and the whiskey and I get a call from Henry in the ER.

At my next appointment Laura tried to get me to talk about my anger at Kate but I honest to God couldn't find any. Maybe if something happens often enough it just doesn't make an impression on you anymore. Eventually, we'll figure it out. Laura's not the type to let these things go.

I ordered a new bed for the house. It's set to arrive on Friday and that's the day I'm moving out. I am.

I love my sister and I've hated her too.

I'm terrified of dogs. Once, when I was little, when my mother was still alive, she sent me down real early in the morning to my grandmother's house to bring her a can of coffee. There were two German Shepherds living across the street and I tried to walk the whole way without making a sound. I knew that dogs have a keen sense of hearing and every squeak of my sneaker soles sent a panicky thump through my chest. Right when I got to my grandparents' front lawn their neighbors' toy poodle came barreling out of nowhere, yapping at me, and I let out this blood-curdling scream and wouldn't stop until the owner appeared, still in her nightgown, to call the little guy off. I was so embarrassed when I handed over the coffee can that I made believe I'd heard some strange yelling too but couldn't see where it was coming from. My grandparents had been down in the basement rehanging a broken clothesline. I was relieved they believed me but annoyed they hadn't bothered to come up and make sure it wasn't me getting bludgeoned to death by some lunatic child-molester.

I'm still terrified of dogs and Laura insists it's really my sister, and in turn my mother, I'm terrified of, how they're dangerous and unpredictable in a menacing, canine way.

I stayed up packing the last boxes the night before I left. The house has two bedrooms and I couldn't shake the impulse to knock on Kate's door and tell her to come live with me. And poor Henry. I felt like I was leaving the two of them alone to maul each other. I told that to Laura and she smiled and said, "Aren't you powerful?"

"I'm worried."

She nodded and said, "Butt out."

Like I said, I've had a lot of therapy and in my opinion it's a rare and gifted therapist who will tell you to butt out.

The next morning the four of us loaded all the boxes into my car and stood in the driveway like I was about to leave for military duty overseas instead of moving to the other side of the island.

"You guys could come over for dinner," I offered.

"No," Kate said, "You spend the time with your friends unpacking and I'll come by tomorrow." She gave me a hug, a tight hug, and whispered into my hair so my father wouldn't hear, "You worry too much."

I drove off thinking that that was one hell of a thing to say, and I was torn between being grateful she knew me well enough to say it and feeling pissed that she had the nerve to say it when she damn well knew I had good reason to worry.

My girlfriends pulled up right behind me and we spent until late in the evening half the time partying, hooking up the stereo first so we could dance, and half unpacking. Cathy made a tray of nachos and we ate on the floor and drank bottles of Amstel Light. There was one bare bulb in the kitchen ceiling because the previous owners took the fixture, and after everyone else left Cathy and I rifled through the unpacked kitchen boxes to find the kettle, mugs and tea. We leaned against the counter waiting for the kettle to boil, then sat out in the square of backyard on my new green plastic lawn chairs. I was sleepy suddenly and closed my eyes, letting the warm minty steam lull me.

"You can make a little pot garden out here," Cathy said.

"I'm gonna get a barbecue," I said, and I saw me in my favorite orange tank top through a cloud of saucy-smelling smoke.

Chapter 3

Thank God for Betsy. Whatever you've heard about evil stepmothers or those poor women who try to replace the original, only to admit a resentful defeat many years later, that was not true for us. Kate and I nearly rolled out the red carpet for Betsy. We knew what we were looking for. We knew what we had had.

By the time Betsy came on the scene we were living in our own house again. I was eleven and Kate was fourteen. My grandmother would be there when we came home from school, but more often than not we'd drop schoolbags, slug a snack and yell our destination point as we tied our sneakers. Kate always had our mother's intensity and by the end of a school day she was nearly bursting out of her own skin. I had more of Henry's disposition and would have been content to watch TV or have a friend over to play The Wedding Game, but there was some unspoken rule between us that we stuck together. Back then I don't think I really knew I was watching Kate. I just couldn't help but follow.

It was a rainy fall day when we met Betsy. We'd been playing Aggravation, popping the dice against the bubble. I looked up and they were standing in the doorway. I'll never forget the shock. I realized in that instant that I had expected her to look like our mother, willowy and maple-eyed, a hint of a fin. Instead, Betsy was plump and pale, sturdy and blond. After they left the room for a predinner Manhattan, Kate dragged me into the foyer coat closet, the two of us clenching our hands over our mouths to keep from laughing, and once in the safety of umbrellas and coat bottoms we burst into peels of muffled laughter.

"She is so fat!"

"She is not really fat, Kate. She's just sort of, I don't know, not skinny."

"She has big boobs. Do you think he's touched them yet?"

"Oh, Kate, gross."

By the time we were called for dinner we had composed ourselves. You could practically see old Henry holding his breath, terrified we were going to pull some stunt.

The truth was, fat or not, she was the first possible mother substitute we'd been presented with and we desperately wanted a mother. We'd talk at night, before drifting off to sleep, about our mother specifications. We had a pretty consistent list for the basic model:

Beautiful
Toll House Cookie Baker
Does not believe in bedtimes
Does not have table manners
Loves Barbies
Hates Catechism
Does not own plastic rain kerchief

We'd add on various accessories as they occurred to us.

"I was thinking," Kate said one night after seeing *The Sound of Music*, "that it would be nice to have a mother who could sing. Then she could sing to us at night."

"We're too old for that, Kate."

"Screw you, May. We are not."

This was an ongoing debate between the two of us. Kate insisted that we were owed all the things we missed out on when we lost our mother, and I felt that we were out of luck. Not that I didn't want those things, but I just felt there were some things you couldn't recover.

Kate kept a running tab of all the things she had coming to her. She wrote it all down in whatever diary she was using at the time. I would find them, under her mattress, in the pocket of her winter coat, and I would read them. "Be in school play so stepmother can attend and take pictures." "Enter school poetry contest. Win, so stepmother can treat me to largest Baskin and Robbins sundae available." "Get caught making out with boy so can get grounded for being bad."

It's not that I didn't feel left out too, but I just didn't see it happening. You can't go back and be a Brownie when all the girls in your class have flown up to Girl Scouts. You'll look like a moron.

Anyway, we pretty much glommed on to poor Betsy from day one. She was ten years younger than my father but always seemed older than him. She drove an old Volvo Station Wagon, periwinkle with black seats. She swam at the Y most mornings and her car smelled of chlorine from the towel and suit she'd leave draped over the backseat to dry. She taught kindergarten at Amelia Earhart on Bay Farm Island and there were always all these egg and milk cartons flapping around in the back boot for her class's art projects. Maybe that's why she seemed so steady, all those needy five-year-olds. And maybe it was just that steadiness that made Kate do the one thing that scared me the most. Test Betsy.

No sooner had Betsy become a constant force in our lives, showing up unannounced to make dinner, an assumed guest at our matinee trips, no sooner did we get what we wanted than Kate started to take it away.

"You leave her alone, Kate," I'd hiss across our dark room at night.

"Fuck off, May. I'm not doing anything to her."

"Are too. You're being mean and nasty and ruining everything for everyone."

"You mean for you."

"And Dad and you too, Kate. I thought you wanted a mother. I thought you liked Betsy."

"She thinks she's so great. She thinks she's better than us. Believe me, May, I'm doing us a favor. You'd go getting all attached to her and she gets sick of us and leaves. Who wants to marry a guy with two daughters? She's not *that* fat. It's not like she has to settle."

"I hate you, Kate," I said, turning away, pulling the covers over my head, but Kate's words hung over me, swaying me. Why would anyone settle for us? Why when our own mother rejected us, left us, tried to kill us? Why should another woman stay?

A few months before my mother drove our car into the bay, she tried to leave without us. It's blurry, like a dream, but I remember her leaning over me while I watched TV, handing me a plate of cut-up apples and starring at me with the bad eyes, smudged slick with mascara.

"I'm going to the store to pick up a few things. I'll be back in half an hour." As she kissed me I looked past her and saw the tan suitcase by the door. The one that had sat open, half-filled on her bed when we got home from school. The one we knew not to ask about—because of the bad eyes. And so I just nodded, watched her scoop up the suitcase and glide out the door. I got up on my knees, leaning on the back of the couch, and stared out the bay window as she got in the car. She turned on the headlights and for a second they blinded me.

"Kate," I called then, afraid to leave the couch, afraid that I would turn and she would disappear. "Kate." My voice rose sharply. She wouldn't answer. Then the car started to back out of the driveway. It made a sucking sound in my mind. And I watched until the headlights disappeared around a corner. Everything pulsed in the silence and I cried out one last time for Kate, "Are you there?" But I couldn't make myself leave the couch. I can't tell you how long I kneeled there, transfixed. I leaned my cheek on the scratchy couch upholstery, rested my head and waited. For some reason I remembered what I'd been told in school about when you're lost, staying where you are so a grownup can find you. Suddenly the house felt so big, I'd get lost. Maybe I fell asleep. Maybe it was as quick as it seemed, but then the headlights swept back into the driveway.

I squinted, trying to make out my mother in the darkness, and when my eyes adjusted I could see her there, a paper cup of coffee in her hand. She was just sitting there, drinking it. I could tell she couldn't see me the way her lips were moving.

You may think I ran out to the driveway, flung open the car door and threw myself into her arms. But I didn't. I watched. I knew, even then, what a deer my mother was, that even her own little girl could spook her. And in my head I chanted, "Hurry, hurry, hurry," to my father at work. "Hurry, please hurry." Because I could feel her going away, a pull in my stomach that told me the car was on and idling.

So when I saw him, like he'd simply appeared, I thought it would be okay. But it wasn't. And maybe I knew that too. When I went into our room, after my father led my mother through the front door and into their bedroom, I found Kate cutting paper dolls, carefully, her brow scrunched up with concentration.

"Didn't you hear me calling you?"

"What?"

Of course, there was no reason for Betsy to care about any of this. She was thirty-four at the time, old enough to worry she'd end up single and alone as the selection of eligible bachelors dwindled to the balding and bizarre but still young enough to have hope.

One summer night, hot air circling my room, the whirl of the ceiling fan lulling me in and out of a prickly heat stupor, I heard Betsy shout, "I will not do this! I will not spend my life paying for her mother!" and my father's urgent murmurs. He must have told her to lower her voice, because from then on all I could hear was the hum of their whispers and then Betsy's car start up in the driveway. The next morning when I shuffled into the kitchen, my father, gray with sleeplessness, sat at the table surrounded by the Sunday paper.

"Is she gone?" I asked simply. He looked shocked for a moment, that I would just come out with it in that way, but then seemed to remember, remember what my life had been.

"Yes"—and he had to look away—"yes, but maybe she'll be back."

I walked past him, digging around in the cupboard for cereal, shaking the boxes to see which one had more than a stale bottom layer of crumbs, and settled on Lucky Charms. The milk was on the table and barely cool from sitting out. When I'd taken a couple bites I said, "I liked Betsy."

Then we heard Kate coming down the stairs, fast and heavy-footed.

"Kate!" my father called, but the front door slammed shut. I got up to go after her but Henry stopped me. "Let her go." And I picked my spoon back up.

It wasn't such a bad idea, really, just letting them both go, leaving Henry and me to our slow, accepting selves, the quiet, the hours melting into one another, so alike. We wandered around that day in slow motion. I pulled on some shorts and a T-shirt and biked down to the beach. It was crowded, toddlers playing, older kids running and squealing in the low tide, their mothers young enough to still wear bikinis. I imagined putting my head in their laps. I'd try on any woman in those days as my would-be mother. There were so many different women that you couldn't know which one might be a good fit. I've heard people say that in love you want to be careful, not to attach yourself too quickly in case it doesn't work out and you get left standing all wide-mouthed with grief. It's different when your mother leaves you because, really, what could be worse? Even now I cling to new lovers like a film, drink in the shine of new love like dew. And when it's over I want to die, know I will break with a snap in two, but I don't. I bend. She gave me that at least.

When I was fifteen I fell in love with Buddy Cane. He was in Kate's class and ran with her crowd. He would show up at our house to pick her up and I'd pretend not to notice him.

"Hey, May," he'd say, flopping onto the couch, "whatcha' watchin'?"

"Nothing. Here," I'd say, tossing the remote into his lap and getting up.

"Hey, May," he'd say as I was heading out of the living room. "Honest to God, I shower once a week, like clockwork, whether I need it or not."

And I'd just roll my eyes at him, go upstairs.

Kate said they never went out, only kissed once, drunk in the sand, but he was around for years, along with the others in her group. Somehow, even though Kate couldn't bounce a ball, she hung out with the jocks, soccer players and girls from the field hockey team and softball team, a couple cheerleaders. The coaches, Miss Jenkins and Mr. Myers, always tried to talk her into joining a sport. Kate had long legs like my mother and just seemed as if she would move fast. It was natural for them to try to recruit her for the track team or tennis. She never said yes. She knew she would fail, knew that in her core she knew nothing about sticking it out, making a commitment and running for a goal as if your life depended on it.

Everyone knew about our mother killing herself and trying to kill us, and I suspect the coaches thought the structure of team sports would give Kate the backbone of responsibility she would need to survive in this world. They didn't understand that Kate hadn't decided whether or not she wanted to survive. She flapped around life like a bat, skittish in the dark, swooping and scary. By her junior year they gave up and turned their attention to me as I entered the ninth grade. Sure, I'd play field hockey. I liked the feel of the stick in my hand and the way my legs ached on the walk home, even the smells of other people's dinners as I walked past each house in the fading light.

"Hey, May, yo-ho!" Buddy was jogging toward me. "What are you? Deaf? I called you three times."

I just stared at him blankly, my mind spinning, making me dizzy. I'd see him out on the soccer field, running endless drills back and forth. Sometimes Kate was there, sitting on the sidelines, drinking a soda or sucking on a Tootsie Pop. Our high school wasn't that big but I did my best to stay away from him. I was sure if I got close to him Kate would detect my interest, use it to taunt and tease me. The thought terrified me. As it was, her group looked at me like some kind of puppy, cute and harmless, maybe something they needed to tend to if it got itself in trouble. Other than that they ignored me.

"You looking for Kate?" I finally managed to say.

"No. I was just with her. I'm just heading home."

"Oh." We walked along in silence for few steps, my mouth getting all gluey and stuck.

"How you liking field hockey?"

"Okay, I guess. I think next year I'm going to try out for goalie. Jen Larkins is a tenth-grader and she'll probably go to varsity next year, so there'll be a space."

"That's cool. I'm a goalie, you know, for the soccer team."

"Oh, yeah, I thought you were," I said, feeling some actual pride at my ability to feign ignorance, act like I didn't secretly chronicle every little snippet of information I could get on him.

"If you want, before tryouts next year, I'll help you practice. It's pretty much the same, soccer and field hockey."

I can't tell you what else we talked about except that I totally clocked in that he missed his block and walked me the whole way to my house.

That next week he kept turning up at school and without even admitting it to myself I started picking out my clothes the night before, although nothing too much to give me away and leave me bait for Kate. We'd smile in the hall.

One day he tossed a baggie of cookies on my lunch table, just yelling, "Want these?"

"Sure," I called after him. My girlfriends stared at me, their eyes buggy. "Shut up," I said to them without moving my mouth. "He's just a friend of Kate's."

If I dressed quickly after practice I could start walking before him and he'd always jog up behind me. Eventually, we just start talking like nothing special. Tests, away games, a teacher of mine he'd had in the past.

"I'm gonna do cross-county track next. You ought to do it. It's brutal but it's cool."

"Yeah," I said, trying to figure if I could conceal my moronness under such close scrutiny, "That might be cool."

"You're gonna have to practice some, start running laps."

And somehow I agreed to meet him in the mornings to run before school.

It was 5:30 a.m. dark, and after two mornings I gave up taking a shower and putting on mascara beforehand. The path we ran hugged the beach and then we'd cross the street and start up Grand Avenue, a wealthy street of huge Victorians, and then circle up Park Street. By the end I was a sweaty smelly mess, but I stopped caring. The early mornings were like another world, soft and whispery. I'd run, listening to our breathing, our breath making puffs of white in the air, our faces growing glistening and pink. By the time track tryouts came along I could run five miles and had found an easiness with Buddy.

Chapter 4

Jack. For starters, I don't trust him as far as I can throw his possessive, illiterate ass.

"Oh, my God, May, I think you're actually jealous of him." Kate laughed. We were sharing a piece of carrot cake at the Buttercup Café, "sharing" being a general sort of term with Kate sucking on the frosting-covered tines of her fork for ten minutes per bite.

"Don't compliment yourself, Kate. I'm just saying that it seems to me like he thinks he owns you or something. Why the hell do you have to check with him to see if you can go to Calistoga with me for the weekend?"

We did this trip every year—just me and Kate—massages, pedicures, mudbaths—the whole thing. I think they pretty much funded their annual remodeling projects from our visits. I'd been squirreling away the money all year. I'd sit at my desk in the library imagining, just tasting the cucumber water in my mouth, brushing the dry crackly mud off my skin.

"Because we might have made some plans for that weekend that I don't remember."

I'm sorry, but she was flat-out lying. "Give me a break, Kate. You don't plan *anything* a month in advance."

"Don't go getting mean, May." The standoff had begun, Kate's eyes shining, clearly pleased. We sat in silence as I stabbed away at the rest of the carrot cake, shoveling it in, and Kate picked at a corner of it like she was prodding roadkill with the toe of her shoe, checking for signs of life.

"Will you stop that?!" I snapped, and her face went all wounded. "Give me a break, Kate." I sighed. "Look, all I'm saying is, why don't you slow down a bit with this guy? You don't know much about him. He's got, what, like a fourth-grade education—"

"Stop being such a mother, May. I'm a big girl. If I want to move in with him, I'll move in with him. And he's dyslexic, not stupid, Miss Snooty Librarian."

"What? Now you're moving in with him. You are *kidding* me. You have got to be so kidding me. Jesus Christ, Kate."

"I love him. And you better stop saying awful things about him because it'll only cause problems later."

"Problems? You threatening me now over this jerk?"

"God May, calm down."

Mumbling, I had my head in my hands, when it occured to me that this little display wasn't doing much to support my denial of jealousy.

I looked up and Kate was giving me one of those mischievous smiles. The kind of smiles beauties get away with every time.

"Does he have an actual job?" I asked, defeated.

"He's the manager at TGI Fridays."

"Oh, well then . . ."

We went to Calistoga—with Kate checking in with Jack like every 20 minutes. Finally, during our pedicures, I grabbed the phone.

"Why don't you just come on up here, Jack?"

"Aw, May, I don't want to intrude on your girl-time."

"Right." I sighed, handing the phone back to Kate.

When I look back at the photos of them at Stinson Beach, with a background of foamy waves and Kate's hair whipped from her face, I admit they look like the perfect couple, in a bliss. Jack had been a jock in high school down in San Diego and he had the ruddy square face and muscular body of a young athlete, even though he was a chain restaurant manager who only occasionally filled in on the restaurant softball team.

When Jack came on the scene I wasn't dating at all, hadn't dated anyone for close to a year. But really that wasn't it. I'd long ago gotten used to the five-to-one boyfriend ratio Kate and I maintained.

I've turned this over and over in my mind—why I was, aside from the jealousy, so suspicious of Jack. After all, he was basically a good and simple guy. I waitressed for years, all the way through college. There's a lot of drinking and drugging that goes on with the restaurant crowd and I'd never seen Jack drunk, never saw him have more than two beers at a time. He worked hard, even lectured Kate on reliability, with uninspired examples of cocktail waitresses overwhelmed in a Friday Happy Hour Hell because some flake called in sick for her shift.

One time I found myself yelling at him that he needed to let up on her, that he didn't understand her fragile nature, and he said, "You need her to be an invalid, May? I mean, I'm just wondering, the way you treat her," which I'm big enough to admit was a pretty smart thing to say, particularly for Jack.

"So, May," he said to me one day when he was over at my house, now so at home he was helping himself to a Pepsi from the fridge, "I know this great guy from the restaurant. He's waiting tables while he's getting his PhD in geology, so of course I think of you—"

"I don't think so."

"Why not? Why don't you just come down to the restaurant for happy hour tomorrow night and I'll introduce you. No big deal."

"Jack, I don't need you to fix me up. You and the other Jell-O shot slingers you hang around with aren't exactly my type."

"That's my point. He's absolutely nothing like me.'

Those were the times I found myself liking old Jack. I mean, who else would say such a thing?

"Okay, Jack. Thanks. I'll think about it. I'll let you know."

"Okay, May, if that's how you want it," he said, all sarcastic, like, "Okay, if you want to be some freaky old maid who collects canaries or something, that's fine with me."

Not long after the beautiful Calistoga trip, Kate and Jack found a garden apartment, a two-story cement rectangle with an admittedly beautiful and lush garden that the owner, Mr. Russo, tended with a loving and maternal hand. Maybe it was Mr. Russo, cooing softly to the doves, plucking the brown spent heads of marigolds, maybe it was the sun-warmed cement on the pads of my feet and the Fifties-style swimming pool filled with splashing children and their squeals, but I felt something comforting and right when I'd visit Kate there, as if the iron swinging gate to the complex would keep her safe. And then there was their love. Kate was flush with the generosity of someone rich with love. For months she told me how she was on time for work, didn't miss a day, didn't curse a single customer. Her boss, Lois, started talking curtain classes and flashed me a wide grin, her eyes darting in Kate's direction, whenever I went to Yards and Buttons to meet Kate for lunch.

Jack took me on like the Holy Grail, teasing, complimenting. He had this way of obviously trying to win me over to his side without insulting me by thinking for a second that I didn't know what he was up to. He made no secret of the fact that he was mad for Kate. I don't know when I'd seen my sister so happy. And it didn't help that Henry and Betsy kept inviting him over for Sunday dinner or along for a matinee. Then Henry handed him a rake one day and I knew I was plain overruled.

"So, May," Jack said on the other end of the phone one Friday, calling me at work, "I just bought us a Weber, some ribs, corn and a bottle of wine for dinner. What do you say you help us break the new barbecue in?"

"You know, Jack—"

"Jesus Christ, May, do you always have to act like I have leprosy or something? You've got to eat dinner."

"Okay."

"Okay?"

"Yeah, okay. I mean, thank you, Jack. That sounds like fun. What can I bring? How about if I pick up some ice cream for dessert?"

"Now you're talking."

He was so clearly and sincerely pleased that I hung up feeling ashamed, thinking, *You really can be such a snob, May.*

I got there around six and the front door was wide open, Jack singing in the kitchen.

"Hey, Jack," I called, "you like Cherry Garcia? I got Cherry Garcia and Chubby Hubby for Kate."

"Yeah, that's cool. You want a beer?" he asked, extending a bottle of Bass Ale. I took it.

"Thanks." And the next thing I knew I'm lounging on the front patio, watching Jack baste ribs while I shucked corn.

A small brown boy was sitting in a puddle of hose water, talking softly to himself, making little splashes in the quarter-inch of water. We sipped our beers and had what I remember to be our first easy talk, time swaying ever so slightly from the heat and the beer, the kids laughing and splashing in the pool.

"So, May, what's up with you and dating? I mean, just so you know, I'm an open-minded kind of guy. I mean, if you're like some kind of lesbo or something, that's cool with me. I mean, really, whatever, it's really cool."

"You are a fucking asshole, Jack. A, I am not gay, and B, with that kind of invitation I sure as hell wouldn't tell you if I was."

"What? What I say?"

"Forget it. You are hopeless."

"So, okay then, if that's not it, then why don't you get yourself a boyfriend? I mean, you're good-looking, May. I know plenty of guys—"

"Oh, no, don't go there again."

"What? My friends aren't good enough for you?"

"They're just not my type, Jack."

"Like, what is your type, May? The invisible type?"

I flung a cob of corn at him, hit him squarely in the stomach. It made a hollow thump and then fell to the ground, rolling into Mr. Russo's rhododendrons. "That's it!" and before I knew it, he scooped me up from the chair and was carrying me toward the pool.

"No Jack. I will kill you," I am screaming, "Put me down now!"

The kids in the pool were all watching us, laughing, and the older ones started chanting, "Throw her in. Throw her in."

"I am not kidding you, Jack. Don't do it."

"You gonna tell me?"

"Get a life, Jack. What the hell do you care?"

"Okay, fine," he said, dangling me over the deep end. The kids were squealing with excitement by then.

"Okay, okay, okay, I'll tell you," I said. "Put me down." And he did. I walked away from him, muttering under my breath, "Jerk."

Jack got us a couple more beers and we fell back into the lounge chairs.

"Look, it's no big deal. I went out with this guy for a long time in high school. We got engaged and then he dumped me, took off for Mexico, and I never heard from him again. That's it. End of story. You happy?"

"Oh, jeez. Hey, I'm sorry, May. That sucks. That really sucks. What an asshole." He was shaking his head, looking like he could just imagine it and it was killing him.

"Thanks, Jack. And I *have* dated some but I just haven't found anyone who's been right, and sometimes I just get sick of trying. You know? Sometimes it's just easier to not get all involved and then have to go through the breakup. You know what I mean?" He was nodding sympathetically and I thought, *I have had just enough beer, thank you, that I'm sitting here spilling my guts to Jack.*

Luckily, Kate came through the gate just then.

"Oh, wow, barbecue. I could smell it from the parking lot and I was thinking, 'Some lucky person is having barbecue tonight,' and it's me!" She dropped her purse at the foot of Jack's chair and fell into his lap, gave him a kiss and turned to me. "You're staying, aren't you, May?"

"Oh, definitely. May brought the ice cream."

"Chubby Hubby," I added.

"Oh, this is the best day. Guess what?"

"What?" Jack and I said together.

"Lois told me today that I can teach the May curtain class."

"All right, baby," Jack said, giving her a squeeze.

"Congratulations, Kate," I said. "I know how much you've been wanting to teach that class."

Kate and I went in the apartment to talk while she changed and Jack put the corn on.

"I am so jazzed about this class, May," she said, kneeling in front of her dresser, flipping through folded T-shirts and shorts. "And on the way out today Lois says to me, 'Good job, Kate, 'cause I totally handled this cranky old hag who was trying to return a zipper she had obviously broken herself. And, May, a zipper costs maybe a buck."

She threw a pink tank and denim shorts on the bed and began to strip, her clothes a pile at her feet. When she turned to face the dresser mirror, pulling her hair up into a clip, I saw it: a bruise the size of an orange on her back, under her right shoulder.

For a moment her voice faded off like I'd dunked my sister in one of those amusement park vats of water. I could see her mouth moving, the sound of bubbles, but couldn't make out a word until she saw the look on my face in the mirror.

"May, are you listening to me?" She turned to face me.

"What's that bruise on your shoulder?"

"What bruise?" She twisted her body side to side to get the right angle in the mirror. "Hmm, God, I don't know." She fingered the bruise, pressing down on it as if testing a cake, and gave the tiniest wince. "I must have bumped into something."

She seemed vaguely perplexed. A moment later Jack called to us that the ribs had maybe five more minutes. Kate flipped her shirt over her head, pulled the shorts up her legs and went out to the kitchen. I just followed. My mind seemed to pulse in and out of the room, couldn't focus on their voices as we passed plates, buttered corn. I caught a glimpse of the bruise again, clearly visible since she was wearing the tank top. And I tried to think. If there were something to hide she sure wouldn't be wearing a tank top.

Chapter 5

Buddy wanted to be a fireman from when he was a kid. His mother, Angela, told me how she never would have gotten him that Radio Flyer fire truck when he was three if she knew what wheels she was setting in motion. By the time he was in high school and still set on this course she started getting up from the couch whenever the news flashed the latest fire story. There were always firefighters getting hurt, or worse, killed, and she had three older boys, knew there was nothing a mother could do to keep a child from a dream.

His best friend, Randy Brouwer, had a father who was a firefighter. A couple times Mr. Brouwer took Buddy down to the station. He told Angela he was trying to help Buddy see the truth, that by talking to the guys at the station he'd understand that firefighting was a dirty and dangerous occupation. Why not get a college education, major in computers? Those kids were making bucks. But Buddy had it bad. He had this book, *Young Men and Fire*, on the nightstand in his room, always open to a different page.

"How many times you gonna read that book?" I'd say when I was over his house, sitting on the bed.

"As many times as I want. How many times you gonna read *Gone With the Wind*?"

"Well, at least that has an actual thousand pages. At least it won a million Academy Awards, and besides, I read other books—"

"Yeah, yeah, yeah," he'd say, pulling me up from the bed, giving me a quick kiss before Angela started calling up the stairs for us, making sure we weren't in Buddy's room with the door closed.

Buddy had two older brothers and they all looked like slightly different versions of their father, Joe, stocky and dark and swaggering. Joe was a foreman at Reed's Construction. On the nights I'd eat over, he'd show up after work, dirty and sweaty, give a quick kiss to Angela and head up to the shower. He'd come down smelling like Dial, in a white T-shirt and jeans. The oldest brother, Mike, was away at college at Cal Poly studying engineering, and the next oldest, Chris, was married and laying carpeting for Carpeteria in Oakland. His wife, Jill, was pregnant when I first met her, and just nineteen. She smiled and laughed more than anyone I've ever met. She was pretty in a straight-blond-hair, full-figured way, and together she and Chris looked like hope. Like anything was possible with enough love and a bridal shower worth of stuff.

She'd waddle into the house for Sunday pasta and seem so genuinely happy to see me, so full of nodding interest and concern, that I started watching her every move, thinking I'd find the secret to her serene contentment.

"What do you think she'll have? A boy or a girl?" I asked Buddy on our run out to the beach.

"A boy. We have a lot of boys in my family."

"What about her family?"

"Boys," he said.

"What do you think we'd have?"

"One of each I guess. If you marry me." And his just bringing it up was enough to make my heart start pounding in my ears, because really I wasn't sure what I wanted. My money was saved and ready to send me to college, and I could see that I would not be having any college if I went and got myself married. Still, that Jill always looked so happy.

"Well, someday I'd like that," I said, "after college."

"I'm not going to college."

"I meant after *my* college."

We were on the beach. Buddy veered off the path onto the sand where the running was harder and I followed. That's all we said about it. I really didn't know what else to say.

But then finally, about ten minutes later when we stopped at the water fountain, I kissed him. "I love you, Buddy."

"Well, then, what's up, May? I mean, I'm not asking you to marry me today. Why are you sounding so cornered? It makes a guy feel real popular."

"Nothing." But even as I said it I knew that wasn't true, and the way he stood there, staring at me, his head cocked to one side, waiting, I knew he was not letting this one go.

"Talk to me, May. What *is* this?"

And then I just burst into tears.

"Hey, hey. Come here. What's up?" He gave me a hug. "What's the matter, May?"

"I need to finish college," I choked out.

"Yeah, yeah. I got that. But what else?"

"I don't know."

"But there's something."

I pulled away then, wiped my eyes and looked up at him, nodded.

"What?"

"I don't know."

"Are you afraid?"

And that made me cry more because just him saying it made me feel anxious in a way so fast and spinning I couldn't catch it to see what it was, like some scary dark phantom, darting in and out of the shadows.

"Come sit down." He put his arm around me and we walked down toward the water, sat down by the shore in the sand.

Buddy fished around for rocks, handed me some, and for five or ten minutes we took turns throwing rocks into the water, hearing them plop. My breathing slowed and I stopped crying, pulled my knees up and leaned my chin on my knees.

"Your mom?" he said finally, like one of the rocks.

"I guess," I replied, "I don't really understand."

"You know what I think? I think sometimes you believe, somewhere inside you, that everyone who loves you is her."

I turned to him then, smiled, and he leaned down to kiss me.

"Come on. Let's head back."

It was my last year of college that the accident happened. I was driving home from school, thinking about what to get Betsy for her birthday, whether I had time for a run before dinner. I walked in the house, threw my backpack on the table and then saw Betsy's face, and just her look moved everything to slow motion.

"What?" I said.

"Come sit down here with me for a second." She took my hand, leading me to the kitchen table. I grabbed someone's leftover glass of water and took a sip. When I put it down she said it.

"Buddy was hurt today. He's gonna be okay, he's alive. Mark Henson died. A house over by the base caught fire, old place that would never have passed code. This elderly couple was living there and the man was trapped inside. Kevin said the woman was screaming, pleading for them to get the old man, and Mark and Buddy went in. The stairs collapsed on their way down and a wall fell on them. They got him out, May, but the wall smashed his arm." She paused then, took a breath. "He lost his arm."

I couldn't say a word, my mouth frozen.

"He's at Alta Bates."

Betsy drove, reaching out every now and again to squeeze my hand, but didn't try to make me talk. I kept thinking over and over about the empty blankness if I had lost him, how Buddy and I were a given, a thing I stopped worrying I'd lose.

He lay, tucked in white, sleeping, and it wasn't until I was standing next to the bed that I could see the flat space where his arm used to be. That's when I stopped thinking about me and started thinking about Buddy. I realized I was crying as if I was watching it happen to someone else.

Oh, God, what is he going to do?

A hand squeezed my shoulder and I jumped slightly, turned to see Angela. We fell together softly, our arms around each other's waists, and never once took our eyes off Buddy. Who knew how long we stood there, but long enough for me to feel her strength seep into me so I stood a little taller and then, finally, the world shook into focus.

"Does he know?" I asked.

"No. He's been sleeping from all the painkillers. He probably won't wake up until morning."

My heart broke off in pieces when each brother, each guy from the station, came to see him, and turned to a crush when Joe rushed into the room. Angela pulled him outside and looked up the two feet of height between them, her voice urging and steady, and I could hear him sob, a choking strange sound. I felt like I was hiding, sinking in a worn white plastic chair by the window. Through the Venetian blinds, I watched slits of cars parking and unparking in the hospital lot.

There must have been fifty people who came in and out of that room that night, and I was thankful for the beeping of the machines and the nurses who floated in with their soft pale hands checking his pulse. He never woke up and I was scared that maybe he was awake, that he was lying there willing himself to die because I knew Buddy. I knew how this would kill him.

Betsy came back around eight that evening with Kate and Henry and a Pyrex dish still warm with chicken pieces, a paper bag of biscuits and a jug of juice.

"Come on," Angela said to me, reaching out her hand. "Let's go eat."

I watched her, talking quietly to my father. She glanced over at me and then nodded to him. Mike and Chris and Randy were huddled together with Randy talking, his arms moving, obviously telling Mike and Chris what happened.

Buddy's sergeant, Kevin Reese, took the empty chair to my right. "Hey, May. How you doing?"

"Did you get him out?"

"What?"

"The old man? Did you get him out?"

"Yeah," he said, "we did."

"That's good."

It was Randy who was with him when he woke up. I was in this daze all night, in and out of dreams where Buddy screamed as he heard the news, crashing from the bed, but what I woke to was Randy tapping my shoulder, saying, "Hey, May, he's up if you want to go in," and I stumbled up from the couch, grabbed onto the doorway to steady myself. Someone had set a plastic cup of juice with a straw on his nightstand, and I focused my eyes on it to walk myself there. He opened his eyes when I sat on the edge of the bed.

I reached down gingerly to hug him, not sure what not to touch."How you feeling?"

"Beat up," he said through a haze of painkillers. "Like a bad fight, like I lost really bad."

"You don't fight."

"Good thing." And he faded off to sleep again.

I got home that afternoon and went directly from the front door to the shower, lost myself in the steam, the water as hot as I could stand it. Sinking to the bottom of the stall, I sat there until the water turned cold. I fell into bed, a deep thick sleep.

I was at the hospital early the next morning. Buddy's family had finally gone home for the night and they weren't back yet. There were seven or eight vases of flowers. I looked at all the gift cards, including one from Tina Morris, Mark Henson's girlfriend. And then I brought the white plastic chair up to the bed, sat there sipping my coffee.

"Hey." Buddy opened his eyes.

"You're one sleeping beauty," I said.

"Damn drugs. Feel like I'm sewn into a mattress."

"Want some of this?" I gestured with the coffee cup.

"Oh, yeah." We got it half in his mouth and half on his hospital gown. He tried to steady himself but couldn't without the support of his left arm. "Shit," he said, falling back. "Shit."

"Here, wait, I'll help you."

"It's okay. It's okay. I can do it, May. Back off," he snapped and I sank back into my chair stunned.

I couldn't even look at him.

He sighed. "Sorry, May. I didn't mean to yell at you."

"That's all right. You have a right to be"—I paused, searching for the word—"frustrated."

"I can't take this," he said, more to himself than to me. "I don't believe this."

"You could have died, Buddy. You were lucky. You could be dead."

"I don't feel so lucky right now, if you want to know the truth."

"Well, sure, not now but later—"

"Like later what? Like later when my arm grows back?"

I swallowed hard, determined not to cry. Angela would know what to say, how to be strong and not crumple under the weight of seeing someone you love in such pain.

We sat there in the silence and then he said, "Maybe you should go, May. Could you do that?"

I stood, slowly pulled my purse from the floor to my shoulder. "I'll come back tonight." I leaned over to kiss him. Even his lips felt strange, hard and scratchy.

Kate was there when I got home, making a sandwich for lunch.

"Want one?" she asked.

"Sure."

"I'm so sorry, May."

"Thanks."

"Come here." She hugged me, tight, and I was crying again, like I had so many tears all you had to do was pinch me for it to start up. "It'll be okay. You'll see. You'll see," she whispered over and over, her hand stroking my hair.

I finally said it. "What if he would have died, Kate? What would I have done?"

"He didn't die, May. It'll be okay."

It was and it wasn't. Buddy went home a couple weeks later. For the first few weeks I'd come by after school and there'd always be Randy or some guy from the station or one of his brothers sitting out back with him, playing cards or watching TV in the living room. Then, at some point, every night there was beer.

"You want another, bro?" Randy called from the kitchen, waving a Miller from two fingers like some rattle.

And before I knew it I said, "He's had enough, Randy."

"What?" Buddy looked up at me.

"I said, you look drunk to me. I don't think you're supposed to be having alcohol with your pain medication. I think it says it right there on the bottle." I angrily scooped his Percocet bottle up from the coffee table. "Or did you forget how to read?" I threw the bottle at him. It hit his chest and he caught it.

I could see Randy standing in the kitchen, the refrigerator door open, staring at me.

"Can we have a moment, Randy?" Buddy called into the kitchen.

"Sure, man. I'll be out back."

We waited until we heard the screen door slam shut.

"For the record, I don't need you telling me when and if I can have a beer. Got it?"

"Oh, yeah? Well, for the record, I don't need a boyfriend who's in a drugged-out stupor every day—and nasty on top of it."

"So then fucking leave if you don't like it, May."

And we stared at each other, eyes all hatefulness and pain.

"That's what you trying to do, Buddy?" I said. "Are you trying to make me leave?"

"No."

"I think you are."

"Yeah, well, I think you want to leave. I think the last thing you signed up for is the one-armed-man circus act."

"You know what? You are one asshole. Don't tell me what I want. What I want is to have back the man I fell in love with." And then I was crying too hard to talk. "Where are you, Buddy? I was so happy I hadn't lost you, but I don't know *where* you are." I tried to catch my breath, waiting for him to reach for me from within this stranger.

"I can't do this," he said.

"What?"

"May, I feel like I've lost everything. All I ever wanted to do was fight fires. I loved it and it's gone. I have nothing."

"You are twenty-two years old, Buddy. You have your whole life. There are other things—"

"Not for me. You know that."

And I did. He was right. I didn't know how you could replace a dream.

"And, May, I think we need to take a break."

"What do you mean, a break?"

"May, this isn't working."

"For who?"

"For me. You fell in love with a guy with two arms and a future. I don't want your pity. I don't want a nurse."

"You're drunk."

"I'm not drunk. I've been wanting to tell you all week."

"But we love each other. Buddy, you're just angry, depressed. That's normal but you'll feel better and then—"

"I don't love you anymore, May."

"What?"

"I said, I don't love you anymore."

"That's not true." I felt like I was falling, so hard and so fast, like a dream where I open my mouth to scream and nothing comes out.

"May," he said quietly, not looking at me, "I said, I don't love you anymore. So, why don't you go? I'm sorry, okay, but you should go."

"Okay," I said, rising, "I'm going."

I drove to the beach with the strangest feeling inside, a feeling that everything was gone and broken, and a relief. I was so tired, like I'd been racing, keeping something upright that wanted to fall down, like to watch it fall let me breathe out.

I sat there until dark, watched planes in the sky, and sailboats, thought about moving fast away. I wondered if my mom was watching me. I thought I see her fin breach the surface, far off where I could barely make it out.

Chapter 6

A week after I saw that bruise the phone rang in the middle of the night.

"May? May, it's Jack."

"What?" I said, my mind struggling to surface from the deep layers of warm sleep to remember who Jack is.

"It's Jack. May, wake up. Is Kate with you?"

I fumbling for the nightstand light, found it finally and switched it on, the light blinding me. "What do you mean, is Kate with me?"

"So, she's not there?"

"No, why would she be here?"

"I don't know. We had a fight last night. Doug, the other manager, was sick and I had to go fill in for him. She was pissed that I was going. I didn't have a choice, May. I tried to explain that to her and she started screaming and yelling. I mean really overreacting. And I get home and she was gone. I figured she'd cool off and come home. But now I'm worried."

"Did you hit her again?"

"What! Are you crazy? What do you mean, again? I would never hit her. Come on, May. Give me a break. I'm really worried here."

And I didn't know whether to believe him or not, although he certainly sounded sincere, scared. "Is any of her stuff gone?" I asked.

"What? I don't know. I didn't look."

"Go check. Go on, Jack. I'll hang on. Go check her closet. See if her purse is around."

I heard him drop the receiver on the counter. I pulled myself out of bed, started pacing a little half-circle around my nightstand.

He finally came back to the phone, sounding breathless."Yeah. Her purse is gone. Some clothes are missing and her suitcase—"

"This must have been some fight."

"It wasn't. We've had worse fights."

"Yeah. I've seen that."

"Seen what?"

"Jack, I saw the bruise on her back."

"What bruise? Are you crazy? Are you trying to tell me that I'm beating up Kate? I mean, I know you think I'm an asshole, but come on, May."

I didn't answer him. I didn't understand why, if they'd just had a fight, Kate hadn't come over here.

"May? Come on. I'm scared. I called Lois and she said she wasn't at work today either."

I couldn't think of what to do except that, if this were just a lovers' quarrel, she'd have been over to my place last night.

"May, I'm really worried." Jack sounded as scared as I was.

"Did you call my dad or Betsy? Did you try her therapist?"

"No. I didn't want to call anyone when I just figured we were having a fight, that she'd come home after one night and we'd work it out. I mean, it's embarrassing calling people, asking where your girlfriend is."

"What time is it?"

"I don't know—about twelve thirty."

"I'll call my dad. I'll call you back in a few minutes."

But she wasn't there. Henry tried to calm me down. "We all know Kate can wax a bit dramatic. It would be just like Kate to *not* call you if she really was looking to worry Jack."

"When I was over there last week she had a bruise on her back," I told Henry.

"What kind of bruise?"

"I don't know, like a couple inches around, like someone punched her in the back." There was a pause where I could hear him breathing, almost hear him thinking.

"May, that's a pretty serious accusation. I know you don't like Jack, but I never got that kind of feeling from him. You know your sister. It would not be beyond her to take off like this. He did say her purse and clothes are gone and—"

"But he could have set that up."

"Okay, May, that's enough. Let's wait until the morning and then if she still isn't home I'll call the police."

I called Jack, told him the plan. We agreed to talk by nine a.m.

Officer Drake arrived within half an hour of Henry's call. Blond and crewcut, he was a young man in his twenties and had an annoying habit of calling me "Ma'am," like I was eighty years old or something. Just having an actual police officer in the house sent a new wave of panic through me. He talked to Jack first, and the whole time I couldn't keep my eyes off him, his badge, his gun, the shiny black shoes and the little pad he penciled notes in.

Jack told him about the fight, her not showing up at work, and Officer Drake asked if she'd done this before.

"In tenth grade," I jumped in, and everyone turned to me. "She ran away for a week in the tenth grade."

"That's right," Henry agreed, and Officer Drake made more notes on his pad.

Then he turned to Henry. "Any drug, psychiatric problems?"

Henry ran through the ream of Kate's therapies, suicide attempts and hospitalizations. Jack found her address book and read off the names and phone numbers of her therapist and psychiatrist.

The cop's nods and soft grunts seemed to change, like it was all coming together for him now. He asked Betsy if she had anything to add to what my father already said.

"No. No, I don't think so, except that she had been doing much better the last six months or so."

"And anything you want to add, ma'am."

"I don't think Kate would run away," I told him, refusing to meet anyone's gaze but Officer Drake's. "I think something must have happened."

"You mean besides her quarrel with Jack?"

"Yeah—I mean, I don't know. We're very close. I think she would have called me if they just had a fight and—" I hesitated, my heart pounding harder. "She had this bruise on her back."

More scratchy notes on the pad. "Did you ask her about it?"

"Yeah. I did. She said she didn't know how she got it."

"Has she been tested for diabetes?"

"What? No. No, she doesn't have diabetes."

"Have you seen other bruises?"

"No."

"Okay. Anyone else see bruises—I'm talking beyond the usual?"

We all shook our heads and Jack sort of sputtered, "Hey, Officer Drake, I just want you to know I know what she's insinuating here and it's not true."

"I'm just trying to give him all the information I can, Jack. I'm not saying you did it."

"Yes, you are, May."

We glowered at each other as Officer Drake stood up. "Okay. I think I have everything I need at this point." He reached in his back pocket, pulled out a wallet and handed us each a business card. "That's my number if you think of anything else. I have to tell you it sounds to me like she took off. But in any case, you can't file a missing persons report until seventy-two hours have gone by. So, I'll call you, Mr. Simpson, tomorrow, first thing in the morning. If she's not back by then I'll put the report in."

Jack walked him to the door, Henry following.

"Can I make some coffee?" Betsy asked, getting up. Jack showed her where the coffee was, and I could see my father out front talking to Officer Drake.

"May?"

I looked over to see Jack, leaning against the doorway, and he was crying. "Oh, Jack—"

"I would never ever hurt Kate. You know I'm crazy about her. I love her. I'm gonna marry her." And with those words he was flat-out bawling. He slumped onto the couch, his head in his hands.

I moved over to sit next to him. "Jesus, Jack, I know. I know you love her—"

"How could you say I'd ever hurt her? How could you say that? What if something has happened to her? What will I do if something happened to her?"

I hugged him, saying, "It's okay. I'm sorry, Jack. I'm just scared. It's okay. It is." I felt like the meanest person in the entire world to accuse him of something like that when he was so damn scared and worried.

Henry came back in the house and headed into the kitchen. I could hear Betsy talking softly and then she came back out to the living room.

"Come on," she said, squeezing Jack's shoulder. "Come have some coffee."

Kate wasn't back by the next morning and by that afternoon I was switching back and forth between wild fantasies of her kidnapping and murder by some serial killer and wanting to kill her myself for pulling such a stunt.

Around three o'clock, Judy, my boss, sent me home.

"I'm fine."

"You're not fine and you're no good to me here," she said good-naturedly. "Go home and take a nap and I don't want to see you here tomorrow either."

"I'm coming in tomorrow. We have that meeting with—"

"May," she said in a tone that stopped me, "if it was me, if it was my sister, I wouldn't be here. Take the time off." The way she said it scared me enough that I opened the bottom drawer of my desk and reached for my purse.

Of course I couldn't nap when I got home so I changed and went for a run. I did my usual course along the beach and then decided to run past Amelia Earhart Elementary. The kids were out for recess and I spotted Betsy, over by the tire swing, pushing three little girls.

Betsy left once, when I was twelve—and I was the one who went after her. Kate tried to make a point of how much better it was with her gone, how we didn't have to eat vegetables at every meal, how Henry let us drink Kool-Aid with dinner, but the truth was, Henry got a call from the school that week that Kate had pulled a big clump of hair out of some girl's head in a fight over a seat at a lunch table. And I heard her up and down at night, not sleeping either.

Somehow, about a month after Betsy left, I found myself riding my bike straight past our house after school, over the bridge to Amelia Earhart. It was three thirty and the last of the buses were pulling out, taking the elementary school kids home. At Amelia Earhart, the classrooms all open to a courtyard. I parked my bike and headed down the walkway, peering in each classroom until I saw her, bent over her desk, cutting shapes out of construction paper—just like she used to do at our kitchen table.

I just stood in the doorway at first without her seeing me. The room smelled like tempura paint and old baloney sandwiches. It was February and she had one whole bulletin board filled with those red construction paper and white doily hearts. The kids had decorated them with sparkles and macaroni and crayons, each kid's name in black marker along one hump of the heart.

"Betsy?" My voice sounded too loud in the empty room. She jumped and then saw it was me. Her face softened in a way that made me start to cry. She got up from her desk and led me over to one of the tables where we sat in the little chairs that were too small for me and way too small for her. I tried to stop crying, but every time I looked at her I cried more because she looked like she was gonna cry too.

"May? Are you okay? Did something happen to your father or Kate?"

I shook my head no, wiping my nose with the back of my hand, and I blurted, "Will you come back, Betsy? I really miss you. I want you to come back. Kate is sorry and Dad is so sad." Just the words made me feel even more desperate, clutchy and scared.

"Oh, May," is all she said. "Oh, May." Brushing my hair out of my face, she handed me a tissue from her pocket. "Come on, sweetie," she said after a bit, "I'll bring you home."

She loaded my bike in the back of her Volvo and I climbed in the backseat, leaning my cheek on the cool dampness of her towel and bathing suit, breathing in the chlorine smell. When we got to our block I couldn't stand it anymore.

"Are you coming back, Betsy?"

"It's not that simple, May. It's more complicated than I think you can understand."

"But you love us, Betsy. I know you love us."

She shook her head, turned around to look at me all glassy-eyed. "Yes, I certainly do."

When Henry came out to the driveway I knew enough to get out of the way. I went up to my room and peered out the window. They were both leaning on the car, their lips moving, and then they walked off together down the block. I watched until I couldn't see them anymore and went down to the kitchen and rummaged around for a snack.

Henry was alone when he came back in the house and joined me at the kitchen table. I knew by the way he was eating his cookie, making crumbs all over the table and floor, that Betsy hadn't gone home to pack her bags. I ran out of the kitchen and up to my room with Henry yelling after me, but I didn't care. I slammed my door. I hated Kate.

But the next day the phone rang while we were eating dinner and it was Betsy.

"She wants to talk to you," I said to Kate.

"About what?" She was all attitude.

"Get up and take the phone," Henry told her.

She yanked the phone out of my hand and went into the dining room, wrapping the cord taunt around the doorway. She came back to the table after a couple minutes. "Betsy's coming over. We're going for Baskin and Robbins. Just me and Betsy." She shoved a forkful of salad into her mouth. "Sorry, May."

"Dad, she's talking with food in her mouth."

It took maybe a month for Betsy to move in and week or two for Kate to test her.

"You know, Kate," Betsy told her, "hate me all you like. I'm not going anywhere." She strode right out of Kate's room. "If this room isn't cleaned up by dinner, no TV tonight." And then she turned back around and slammed Kate's door, before Kate had a chance to do it.

I wanted to let out a little whoop but kept my head down, shoving the warm folded towels into the linen closet.

Chapter 7

Cathy was in town for the week. She's a ranger up in the Sierras, so I only see her five or six times a year when she comes down or I go up. It was one of those heat-wave August days and we were in our bathing suits, lying in lounge chairs, squirting ourselves with a water bottle every fifteen minutes. Cathy's pretty much my oldest friend in the world. We were in Mrs. Bastow's fifth-grade class together. Cathy's family had just moved from Colorado so they didn't know anything about my mother—yet. I knew, at some point, one of the other mothers wouldn't be able to help herself from telling Mrs. Lane what had happened. I'd see them, all huddled together whispering, waiting to pick their kids up after school. They'd stop when Kate and I walked by, look at us all sad-eyed. I'd ignore them but Kate sometimes couldn't do it. She'd stare back until they looked away.

Sure enough, right before Halloween, Cathy asked me, "So what happened to your mother?"

You took your chances, back then, when you asked me that question. It was a question that instantly put me on the defensive. Having to tell people what my mother did, and tried to do, made me feel ashamed, like somehow, by being her daughter, it was my fault too, or said something about me—my sanity, my morals, my worth. Sometimes Kate would use my mother's death, and what she'd done, to get out of a science project. She'd burst into tears, saying she was too upset to concentrate. And the truth is, some mornings Kate would come down to breakfast and look not right, pasty and smoldering, distracted, and you could pretty much count on those being the days she'd cut out of school or get sent home for a fight or mouthing off to a teacher or hall monitor. Still, sometimes she played it for all it was worth. I'd be a little more self-righteous about it except that I did it a bit myself, hardly ever, really, but I have. You almost can't help it. When you're the daughter of a suicidal and murderous mother people treat you like some kind of pariah when they hear about it. It was this excuse, this shiny hanging fruit you rushed up and plucked, only to feel sick with it later.

"She drowned last year," I told Cathy, "and Kate and I were in the car. But we got out."

Confused, Cathy looked at me, her lips pressed together. "I heard she tried to kill you."

"I guess she did," I said, looking straight at her, the little hairs on the back of my neck all standing up.

"Were you scared?"

"Yeah, scared." She looked so scared herself I had to look away. "And then there were all these men running around and the ambulance," I said slowly, seeing it, like I always do when I talk about it, "and the boy."

"What boy?"

"There was a boy in the back of a truck. I saw him. He looked like he was going to cry."

There's probably not a week that goes by that I don't think about that boy, the way he looked at me like he was me, the little wave as I got in the ambulance. I figure I'll never know who he was and where he is now. When you share the worst moments of your life with a stranger he becomes something else, not a stranger, but not anyone you know either, just someone you want to see again.

That's all we said then, went out and played, me pumping hard and high on the swings outside.

"I think," Cathy said, sitting up in her lounge chair, wiping her face with a towel, "she's just doing one of her Kate things. Jack's probably telling the truth. You know, it would be just like her to throw a fit when she doesn't get the attention she wants, when she wants. And for whatever else you think of Jack, he draws the line on her drama when it interferes with work. Remember, last Thanksgiving, when he had to work? I was there when she started in on him and he told her right off, 'I work for a living, Kate,' and she stormed off, but he worked Thanksgiving."

"Yeah, I know. I mean, it's the kind of thing Kate would do. But she's never done anything this big before—"

"What are you talking about? What about the time that other boyfriend—what was his name? The one with the tattoo?"

"Hal."

"Yeah, Hal. Remember, when he cheated on her with that gal at the Walgreens. She took that whole bottle of aspirin—"

"Sure, but she didn't disappear. That's what I'm saying. Kate usually does something where she can see right away that she's fucked everyone up. She has no idea what we're doing. We could all be going on like nothing happened, for all she knows."

"But she knows you wouldn't."

"I know. But still. You get my point."

"I suppose."

I took a sip of my lemonade, which was all diluted from the melted ice and barely cool. "And last night I was remembering something I forgot to tell Officer Drake. The day before I saw her bruise I bumped into her in the Walgreens over by the pharmacy section. I just figured she was picking up one of her prescriptions, but when she saw me she came right up to me, all hyper and cagey. I almost asked her if she was okay. I didn't, but I almost did. And then she left."

"Yeah?"

"I mean she just left, without getting anything."

"Oh."

"I think that's weird. I think she was getting something she didn't want me to see."

"Like what?"

"I don't know. Something."

The phone rang and I reached for the portable I had lying in the grass next to me.

It was Jack.

"She went to New York."

"Jack? What do you mean?"

"I just got home from work. I'm standing here holding a United Airlines itinerary showing a round-trip ticket to JFK."

"Why would she go to New York?"

"Damned if I know. I just called the airline and checked, though. She used the ticket."

"Christ."

I was so angry. *So Kate. So friggin' Kate.*

"Who does she know in New York?" he asked.

"No one. We don't know anyone in New York."

"Well, at least she's alive," he said, but finally, he sounded angry too.

"I'm sorry, Jack."

"Me too—"

"No, I mean I'm sorry for thinking you did, you know, anything. I was just worried and scared but that wasn't right."

"Ah, don't worry about it, May, but thanks. I know you can get a little freaky when it comes to Kate."

"I do not think—"

"Joking. Joking. Just trying to bring a little levity to the situation. What are you doing tonight? You want to go get a drink or something? I could use a drink."

"Cathy's in town. We were going to shower and go out to dinner. You want to come?"

"No. No. I don't want to crash your girl thing. We can do it some other time."

"You sure? It's really—"

"Nah. I'll take a rain check."

"Take care of yourself, Jack."

"Poor guy," Cathy said, getting up, shoving her towel and squirt bottle into her bag. She shook her head. "Kate strikes again."

"Why would she go to New York?" I said again.

"You know, May, I love you but you spend way too much time worrying about Kate. Kate has her problems and she's going to do, whatever she's going to do and in the fifteen years I've known you I've seen you let Kate drag you around with her crises. And every time, you know what? She ends up fine and you end up bruised."

"I know," I said wearily, almost ashamed, because at times like this I could picture myself a little girl again, clinging onto Kate as the only thing I had left, like something I can't help but do.

"I'll be back in an hour. And then let's go swing by and pick up Jack."

"Okay," I said, smiling. That's the thing about Cathy, solid as can be, but a big old squishy heart inside.

After Buddy broke up with me I lay on top of my bed the whole next day, and the day after that, and then the day after that Cathy was standing in my bedroom doorway. She hadn't even been in town. She was in ranger school at the time, up in the Siskiyou National Forest. She said when she called me from the only pay phone at the camp that week, she heard a flatness in my voice so unfamiliar that she was determined to make the five-hour drive.

"Hey," she said, coming to sit. I picked my head up from the bed and caught a glimpse of us in the mirror—me with my hair all stringy and tangled, looking on the outside how I felt on the inside, and Cathy, all taunt and serene in her uniform like some freshly made bed.

"You didn't need to come down here. I'm fine."

"Yeah," she said, "it sure looks that way."

I rolled my eyes, gave her a shove. But I got up and showered.

And while I was showering she said, "The Alameda Fair is tonight."

"Yippee."

"I think you should go."

"Okay, if you want to go."

"I think we should double-date."

I stuck my face around the shower curtain to look at her. "What're you talking about? We don't have anyone to double-date. I just broke up with Buddy and you don't have a boyfriend."

"I brought a couple guys down from the camp with me."

"You did *what*? Jesus, Cathy, I don't feel like going on a blind date tonight."

"May, just listen. They heard I was coming down here to see you, and I talk about you, so Josh and Jerry were like, 'Hey, we'll come cheer her up.'"

"You told them?"

"It's nothing to be ashamed of, for God's sake. People break up."

I turned off the water, started drying off. "No."

"May."

"No. Sorry. You should have checked with me first."

"You would have said no."

"You're right."

"May, look, it's no big deal. They know you're on the rebound. No one's going to be pulling out any engagement rings or anything, and the beauty is, tomorrow they're gone. They don't even live around here. Jerry's from San Bernardino and Josh is from Suisun."

When I sighed, she glanced back at me, sheepish but pleased.

That night I went downstairs, dressed for the first time in days, and Henry and Betsy were watching a video, eating some popcorn in the den.

Henry clicked the pause button when he saw me. "Going out?" he asked.

"Yeah. I'm going to the fair." I shrugged.

"And you look really happy about it, too."

"Cathy," I said, "Cathy set it up. We're going with these two guys from her camp that I don't even know."

Betsy let out this little involuntary laugh and almost instantly stifled it. "That's a good friend."

It was seven o'clock with still plenty of light when we got to the fair. Two rows of vendors lined Park Street and I could smell barbeque and popcorn from somewhere I couldn't see. Josh was taller than Cathy, his wavy brown hair cut short, and he was young, nineteen. Jerry was older, our age, and wore these khaki shorts and round metal glasses like Indiana Jones. They were both nice enough, except I didn't know what the hell Cathy had told them. They treated me like an egg, too breakable to travel well. They walked on either side of me, and finally I couldn't stand it and picked up the pace so it didn't look like they were taking me out for my first walk since the lobotomy.

"Anyone hungry?" Josh asked as we approached the meat-on-a-stick booth. We decided to pass on the meat and kept walking in search of the plates of Chinese food we'd seen this family stroll by with. When we got our food we went to sit at one of the large round tables set up near a band playing country music. At first we were just eating, drinking sodas, and I thought, *This is okay*, that it was good to get some night air and that Cathy was right, Josh and Jerry were easygoing, just along for the ride.

"Hey, May, Josh and I are going to go over to that booth with the cowboy boot footstools. You guys want to come?" It finally occured to me that maybe Cathy had wanted Josh and Jerry to come because she liked one of them.

"That's okay. I'll wait here."

"Me too," Jerry said. They headed off down the street and the band took a break. "I needed this."

"Yeah?"

"Yeah. It's hell, and boring, at the camp. Don't get me wrong. I love being in the woods. I'm lucky to be there, but seeing the same people day after day and that lousy food, it gets old."

"I could see that." I nodded. "So, you want to be a ranger around here?"

"Hell, no. I'm hoping to go somewhere where there's some big national forests—Montana, Wyoming—that kind of thing. You ever been to Wyoming?"

"No."

"Sky. Nothing but sky, and at night, a million stars."

"That sounds nice."

"Yeah, it is. You should go sometime."

"I should."

We ate quietly for a bit, watched the people. I saw some people I knew—Alameda is a small town in a lot of ways—but I kept my head down when I did. I didn't want to talk to anyone that night. They'd only ask about Buddy and then I'd have to act like nothing had happened or say we broke up, which didn't seem like something I could do.

"I'm sorry, by the way, about your boyfriend. I mean, about his arm and your breaking up. That's rough."

"Thanks."

"Cathy said not to say anything but I can see you're sad."

"Thanks, Jerry."

He smiled awkwardly.

"You have a girlfriend?"

"No. Not now. I figure I'll be moving before the year is up. I don't want to get involved and then have to deal with that when I'm transferred. And you don't want to be dating the girls at the camp. Too weird. Ends up feeling like you're dating your sister, or your cousin."

That made me laugh a little and Jerry looked all pleased with himself.

Just then the band started up again, a swingy number.

"You want to dance?" Jerry asked.

And I actually did.

It was starting to go dark and in the purplish pink of dusk, the vendors switched on tiny white Christmas lights. We danced among swaying, jumping three-year-olds and one older couple who actually knew how to dance and five people dancing in a group. I caught the eye of the guitarist and he winked at me in a happy way that made me smile. Then past him I saw Randy, and when he reached down to pick a wooden box off a table, I spied Buddy. He was talking to Randy and picking up another of the boxes, talking to the vendor. Just then the song ended and I started to walk back to the table. But another song started, a slow song, and without even asking, Jerry pulled me close. A woman was singing this time, one of those love-lost country songs I make fun of that are never good to hear when it's happened to you. I closed my eyes to keep from crying and somehow ended up with my head resting against Jerry's shoulder. When I opened my eyes Buddy had seen me, and from the look on his face I suddenly realized what it must look like, me and Jerry, and the slow song, but I froze. Jerry turned us around and I was facing away.

"You okay?" he asked.

"Yeah. Yeah. That's him. Don't look. Over there. That's Buddy."

"Is he watching us?"

"Yes."

But when I twisted my head to look for him he was gone.

I stayed up the whole night that night, knowing what he must have thought, and by ten o'clock the next morning I was at his house.

"He left early this morning, May," Angela said, leading me into the house and handing me a cup of coffee. I sank into one of the kitchen chairs.

"Left for where?"

"Mexico. Randy has a friend, some guy named Hawke, who does fishing down there, and Buddy's going to go down and help him out, give it a try."

"He's leaving me to be a fisherman for some guy named Hawke?"

Angela sat down next to me and took my hand. "Honey, I don't think he's so much leaving you as trying to find himself."

"You know," I said softly, unable to even look at her, "that he doesn't love me anymore?"

"May, he doesn't know what he feels right now. You know more than anyone that Buddy lived to fight those fires. He's angry and scared and lost. He's not good for anyone right now—not you, not himself. And he won't listen to anyone. I think he had to go."

Chapter 8

It was one of those Indian Summer October days, days of sundresses and runs I did early before work or eight o'clock at night when the sidewalk started to cool. It'd been almost three months since Kate left, disappeared, whatever it was that she'd done, and I still had mornings when I woke up and forgot something terrible had happened until I got the toothpaste on the toothbrush on the way to my mouth. It made me jump inside and my forehead go hot, but I stepped up and out of it now, like some muddy hole I'd found myself in.

On Saturday morning I parked in front of Java Rama, stuck some quarters in the meter and headed inside. It was early enough at nine thirty for the place to be only partially full, a lovely quiet feeling of waking up, with people talking softly and the smell of coffee and pastries. There were studying students and their drained giant mugs of lattés, and two mothers, each with a stroller. Betsy was sitting toward the back by the window. She was wearing the pale blue sweatshirt with the rainbow fish she bought years ago on a trip we made to Cape Cod when Kate and I were in junior high. Her hair was still damp from her swim, shiny with the film of gel she runs through it with her fingers.

"I just this second ordered you a tea," she said, getting out of her chair to hug and kiss me and retrieve the tea and her coffee from the counter.

"Perfect." She'd also ordered a cherry cheese danish and some kind of scone. For a minute or so we said nothing, passing sugar and cream, stirring, staring out at the side street.

"So," she began, "are you relieved about Jack?"

It wasn't exactly relief I felt that day when I hung up with Jack—or maybe it was, some other kind of relief. But still. It didn't answer why. Why would Kate want to make herself disappear? Why would she leave without telling me?

"I guess." I hesitiated. "I mean, it's better than them saying she's probably dead, isn't it? How do you feel about it?"

"Protective, I guess, of you and Henry. Angry for your pain. Annoyed with Kate that she would pull such an immature stunt at her age, just when I thought she was getting better. Like a fool for thinking she was better. Probably other things. I don't know . . ."She broke off a piece of scone, then broke off a smaller piece and ate it. "I like to think I know people and I have to admit, now, I don't know Kate."

That stopped me, my mug partway to my mouth, because that's what I felt, a kind of betrayal. I've always felt that Kate and I are almost one, that that day we emerged from the freezing water, from death itself, we were reborn in some special way that bound us together for life, that saving each other from our own mother created something akin to an amniotic bond. So, for Kate to choose to leave, to not have been taken, somehow broke a rule. In the same way that every time she tried to commit suicide she was breaking the rules. I looked up at Betsy. "I guess you're right. I guess I didn't know her either, I guess."

Betsy smiled sadly at me, reached over, in that way she had, and squeezed my hand. "I think, though, she'll be back."

"Why?"

"For you."

"Maybe," I scoffed, but I was fighting back tears just the same.

"Betsy?" a voice called from the counter. Betsy glanced past me and I turned to see a man in his forties—khaki shorts, T-shirt, boat shoes, his hair sandy and curly—walking toward us.

"Hi, Scott," Betsy said casually. "Getting some coffee?"

"Yeah, just trying to get going before I pick up Morgan from her mother's."

"Scott, this is my daughter May."

"Hi, May. Nice to meet you finally. I've heard a lot about you. You're one of the children's librarians at the Alameda Library, right?"

I tried not to show my surprise. I sort of remembered Becky mentioning him. "You teach kindergarten, too, don't you?"

"Fourteen years. We should hook up. I've been meaning to get my class over there." He smiled.

A guy with red spikey hair yelled, "Double cap!" from the counter.

"I'll be right back," Scott said.

"Now *he's* a very nice guy," Betsy whispered, leaning across the table. "I don't know why I never thought to introduce you," she added, almost to herself. Then Scott returned. "Can you sit?" she asked.

"Sure." He looked at his watch. "I've got a couple minutes." He pulled a chair from another table and sat down.

"Scott's a cyclist," Betsy said in a suddenly chipper voice.

Oh, my God, Betsy.

"You ride?" he asked.

"I run."

"Yeah, I run too. You kayak?"

Yeah, I'm like the Iron Woman of Alameda, I wanted to say. "No. Is it good?"

"It's unbelievable. You've got to try it. You too, Betsy. You'd love it."

"Okay," she said. "Maybe you can take us out sometime."

Slow down, Betsy.

"Sure. That'd be great. So, I finally had to call Cody Massen's mother on Friday." The two of them started blessedly talking work. I cut the cheese danish in half and ate it, smiling and nodding, but not really listening to them, more checking out old Scott to see what I was going to tell Betsy after he left and she asked if I wanted her to have him call me or invite him over for dinner. He seemed nice enough and cute enough, and as long as he didn't think we were going on some triathlon for our first date, we could go to dinner or something.

"I better get going," he said. "Gail's got a hair appointment, so she wanted me there a little early to pick up Morgan."

"What are you guys going to do today?" Betsy asked.

"We're gonna take a bike ride and then go get her some sneakers and then I don't know. I play it by ear. See what she's up for."

Betsy couldn't help a smug little smile as if to say, "Isn't that nice."

All right Betsy, sold! Honest to God. Really.

Betsy watched him head out the front door and said, "I think I'm going to invite him over for dinner."

I stopped at the Safeway afterward, picked up groceries and drove home actually hoping that Scott would ask for my number. I try not to really think about it but the fact is I don't date much. I haven't dated much since Buddy. Yeah, I know that's been like three years, but you'd be surprised how fast the time goes when you don't really like dance clubs and drinking to begin with. Betsy will tell you that's no excuse. She was older than I am now when she met my father and she never once set foot in a bar in the pursuit of a relationship. They met through friends, which I think is one of the reasons why Betsy is so hot to always fix me up, like it's her chance to give back. There was this guy a couple years ago, the son of her friend Anne, Jamie, who was pretty nice. He was also a librarian and did some running, so Betsy and Anne were one step away from drafting wedding invitations. But then it turned out he was gay. It was okay. Somehow our dating finally pushed him to face facts and come out.

The night he told me we were sitting in Just Desserts after seeing *Toy Story*. It was maybe our sixth date and he said, "Listen May, I need to tell you something." He looked so worried I thought he was going to tell me he had cancer or was going to jail.

"Sure. God, Jamie, what's the matter?"

And he told me.

I just stared at him for a minute, trying not to look shocked that he just blurted it out like that, and after a few seconds I regained my senses and said, "Really?"

"Yeah."

"Okay."

"I mean, I'm sorry, May. You're a really nice girl—woman, whatever—and I didn't ever mean to—"

"Hey, it's okay, Jamie."

"No, it's not. You think you're going out with some guy who'll maybe marry you and you want to have kids and here I am wasting four months of your life."

"Jamie, it's cool. Really. It's a relief. I mean, you never really seemed, you know, into the sex part and I was sort of getting a complex that it was me—"

"Oh, no, it's not!"

"Well, obviously not now, but I knew something was up. Does anyone else know?"

"These two women I'm friends with at work and this guy Mark, who they introduced me to, who works over at U.C. Berkeley and is also gay."

"Not your parents?"

"No."

"You gonna tell them?"

"Yeah. I mean I think they know really. But, yeah."

"Well, good for you, Jamie."

And he smiled at that. "So you don't hate me?"

"No, come on, how can I hate you? You're too nice of a guy. If you're up for it I'd like to stay friends."

"I'd really like that too."

And now Jamie and Rich are partners and are two of my closest friends. That's where I was going that night. They just adopted a little boy, two months old, through the foster-adopt program, and we'd planned a baby shower at their place. I was making my goat cheese strata.

I realized as I pulled into the driveway that I forgot to pick up wrapping paper for the present. I got them one of those bouncy swings that hang from a doorway. I'd have to go back out after I unpacked the groceries. I collected the mail from the box at the end of the driveway and shuffled through it—phone bill, circular, my *Vanity Fair.* And then I saw it, a postcard. I knew her handwriting before I could focus my eyes enough to read it. *Don't worry. Love, Kate.* That was all. I looked for the postmark. It was stamped Southampton, New York. I didn't know anyone in Southampton, New York. I had no idea where Southampton, New York, actually was.

I carried the groceries inside in a sort of daze, lined the bags up on the counter and then sat down on a kitchen chair to catch my breath. My heart was beating like a wild woman's. *Jesus, Kate. Is this some kind of a joke?* So now I knew she was, or had been, in New York. And obviously, unless she was spending her days wrapped in a sheet, shaking a tambourine in JFK, she was there under her own will. *Fuck her. Just fuck her.* I threw the postcard on the table and started angrily unpacking the groceries. Who the hell did she think she was anyway? *You can't bother to just make a friggin' phone call, let people know where you are? Don't worry, Kate. You're not such a ray of sunshine that we can't get through a day without your presence. No one's going to go flying off to New York to force you back.* Did she even have refills on her medication? I thought Southampton was on Long Island. *There's a lot of water around there. I think it would be a perfect place to drown yourself. Forget it. Just forget. She's an asshole.*

I dialed Betsy and Henry.

"I got a postcard from Kate," I told Henry when he picked up.

"So did we," he said wearily.

"From Southampton. What the hell is she doing in Southampton? We don't even know anyone in Southampton. We don't know anyone in New York. Do we?"

"Well . . ." He hesitated.

"What?"

"Your mother and I used to have a friend in Pennsylvania, near where I grew up."

"How could Mom have a friend in Pennsylvania? She grew up in L.A."

"Mostly. But she did a year of school at Bryn Mawr. That's how we met."

"You never told me that."

"No? Well, it was a long time ago."

"I thought you met when you moved out here to go to Berkeley."

"No. No. We met in Bryn Mawr. Anyway, that's pretty far from Southampton. I don't know anyone in Southampton."

"What should we do?"

"May, I don't think there's really anything we can do. For whatever reason, your sister wants to be somewhere where she can't be found. She's an adult—"

"Barely."

"But she is, and this is her choice."

We hung up soon after that. I started making my strata, put on some music. *Let it go, May.* But of course I couldn't.

Chapter 9

Date with Scott tonight. I've decided Scott is actually handsome in an Indiana Jones kind of way—the scruffy, khaki, power-bar-eating, beatup-two-hundred-plus-mile-Toyota-Civic kind of look. Which I don't think has ever really been my kind of look, but since I've only dated three guys in the last eight years I might not be an actual expert on what my type is. We're going to the old San Rafael Theater to see *Harold and Maude.* Scott appears to be the only person on the planet not to have seen *Harold and Maude* but then I made a fool of myself by not really being able to tell him what it's about since it's been ten years since I've seen it. Before that we're going for sushi. Of course, when you never go out on dates you realize you have nothing to wear, so three hours before he's supposed to pick me up I was in Macy's throwing sundresses into the arms of a very sympathetic saleswoman. She was maybe eighteen and watching me like some kind of *National Geographic Special*—"Women Who Seldom Date." If I'd had any more time I would have been indignant and embarrassed, but really there was no time for such luxuries.

"What do you think?" I asked her, emerging from the dressing room in a tiny green and white checked number that I think makes me look a little like Maria von Trapp in the curtains.

"Fallback position," she said.

"What?"

"Keep it on hold. Let's see what the others look like." She was so serious, I flung myself back into the dressing room, my heart pumping.

"Okay, what do you think?"

"You know what would look really so cool with that? Doc Martens. You have Doc Martens?"

"Emily, do I look like the Doc Marten type to you?"

"Strictly Land's End?" she said like she was playing Fashion Trivial Pursuit.

"You got it."

"Let's try the next one."

We settled on a pale blue dress, fitted on the top and with a wide skirt. I had shoes that would match it at home. It was Audrey Hepburnish without being too formal, which of course you don't want to be when you're out with Indiana Jones, right?

Unfortunately, when I got out of the shower, did my hair and tried the dress on again it looked way too big. Not like a size too big, but just too much dress. I brushed against the side of my nightstand and knocked my clock to the floor.

"Shit!" I hissed, throwing open my closet door. "Shit, shit, shit!" But really I have nothing else but workclothes—with entirely too many little animals and Disney characters on them, I realized—and jeans. Scott would be ringing the bell in fifteen minutes.

For one fleeting moment a wave of relief washed over me as it occured to me that I could cancel, that I could develop a terrible and debilitating migraine, but then I realized it was too late and he was probably on his way.

Aargh! Door knocking! He's early!

I pulled the mascara wand out of its tube and accidentally ran it along the whole side of my hand.

"Shit, shit shit!" *Forget the mascara.*

I could develop food poisoning from the raw fish halfway through dinner.

I slammed my bedroom door closed and ran for the door, stopped in front of it and took two slow breaths. *Knock, knock knock!! Ahhhhh!*

Love sake. Warm, soothing, light, fragrant. And Scott ordered a Sapporo so I had the dainty little ceramic pitcher all to myself. We sat at the bar where boats of sushi sailed by and we reached out for one dish after another, though you don't want to actually stare at the dishes because that can make you a bit dizzy—if you've drunk most of your sake.

"Betsy's great. You probably know I was her student teacher."

I nodded, which technically didn't count as a lie if you wanted to be technical about it, and what with the Scarlett O'Hara dress and the soothing effects of the sake I was feeling all demure and Miss Manners. I didn't have the heart to tell him I had never heard of him before that morning in Java Rama.

"She used to always talk about you and your sister. She just adores you guys, but you probably know that."

"Well, we adore her."

"Yeah, we kept saying we'd get together outside of work. But you know how that is with a kid and all. It's hard to get out, especially when they're young."

I picked up the sake pitcher to pour myself some more, realizing that I'd drained the damn thing already, and tried to put it back down without him recognizing me for the lush that I am.

"You want another," he said.

"Oh, no!"

"Sure? 'Cause I could have another beer."

"No. No really. I don't drink much," and even as I said it, I was noticing how the little sushi boats were just the tiniest bit blurry. I had to look away 'cause I was getting this seasick feeling watching them.

He didn't ask me anything about Kate, even though I could tell he knew. Betsy probably told him everything, judging by the way he side-stepped every time the conversation threatened to veer in that direction. More than once I thought how weird it was to be out on an actual date without Kate around to tease me or eye my outfit. Still, part of me hoped he'd ask about her so I could talk about her and my anger. It goes together like that; Kate and my anger, and the hurt and the fear, are right there if you peel back the surface. And really, did I want to get into that with a guy I didn't even know? I did. I'd get into it with the Fed Ex man who comes into the library every day at two o'clock if I was given the chance. But, like I said, Scott didn't ask. On the way home from the movie he said, "That was really fun, May. You want to maybe go out kayaking next weekend or something?"

It was dark enough in the car that I don't think he saw me jump ever so slightly in my seat.

"Um, sure. I think so. I mean, why don't you call me during the week 'cause I don't remember what I have planned next weekend."

This weird silence ensued as I realized how cagey I sounded.

"You don't really want to go out again, huh?"

"No. No. It's not that at all. It's probably fine. I'm just saying that I don't have my actual datebook in front of me. I think I even left it at work and so I can't tell you for sure—" I could hear myself babbling on like one moron. I took a deep breath. "Okay. Yes. Let's just say yes and then I'll call you if there's some kind of problem, okay?" *Oh my God!*

He pulled the car in front of my place, turned the engine off and looked at me like he needed to rummage around in the glove compartment for my medication. "Okay, May. Great. Are you okay?"

"Fine!"

"Great. Well, thanks again for a really nice evening."

"Yeah. Thank you, it was fun."

Then we just sat there, nodding at each other like two Weebls. I was not kissing him good night, okay? I barely *knew* him. And then I thought of calling Cathy when I got in the door and could almost see her rolling her eyes and yelling, "Jesus Christ, May, just get a friggin' habit and get it over with already!"

I inhaled like I was taking a dive, lunged across the seat at him and kissed him *on the cheek*.

I was walking up to my front door, my insides chanting, *That counts. That does not count. Oh, yes, it does. You are pathetic.* I tried to block out the glimpse of Scott's shocked face I caught as I threw myself out of the car and slammed the door, taking two steps away only to turn around and start waving good-bye like some ADHD four-year-old.

I went straight from the front door to the bathroom and started a bath. *Never again. I do not need to do this to myself. I am fine. I am my own person. Lots of amazing women stay single, live full and happy lives, do not become lesbians, do not resort to raising apes like Jane Goodall. Whatever. I am not doing this again. I just am not.*

It was cold in my room when I woke up. I jumped out of the bed, slammed the window shut and hopped back in bed, pulling the covers tight around my neck. It was a couple weeks before Daylight Savings Time ended and the mornings stayed dark until almost seven a.m. I glanced over at my alarm clock, nine a.m. and then out the window where the branches of trees flailed about in the wind and the sun made bright yellow steaks between the leaves. Probably that was it, the way the sun hit the leaves, the fall colors and kissing Scott, but right then I could see Buddy's face that first time he proposed, clear as if he was sitting on the edge of my bed, smiling his crooked smile, shaking his head, saying, "Oh, May. May, May, May," like he would when I'd stayed up all night studying for an Intro to Psych class and slept through my alarm, leaving him standing on the corner of Central and Grand, done with his stretches and ready to run.

That morning he proposed Betsy was already up, starting waffles, and let him in. When he gently pushed the covers from over my head it felt like a gush of wind swept into my bed and I jumped.

"Hey," he said.

"Oh, no." I glanced at the clock. "You must have been standing out there forever."

"Half-hour."

"I can be ready in a sec."

"Nah. Let's go later." He lay down next to me, his head propped in his hand. "Betsy's making waffles."

"Okay," I said, rubbing my eyes.

"Hey, May—ah, forget it."

"Forget what?"

"Nothing. Whatever. No big deal."

"What? Come on, Buddy," I said, feeling fully awake now and curious.

"Well." He looked so damn serious, getting up and then sitting down again, I knew it was something really bad.

"Did you get fired?"

"No!"

"Is somebody sick? Oh, God, are you sick?"

"Jesus, May, calm down, you're making this harder. Kate's right, you do worry too much." He looked away, and then back at me and then away again and finally said, "It's just I was thinking—like for the past couple days I keep having this thought and so this morning I was thinking maybe we could talk—don't look at me like that, okay?"

"What?" I couldn't help it. I was laughing at him, which made him blush a little and stand back up.

"I was just thinking maybe, now that I'm out of training and off my probationary period at the station, that maybe this would be a good time to—to get engaged, okay? That's all. I was just thinking that maybe that would be a good idea."

"Oh," I said, and I realized I had my hand over my mouth like someone had just told me something terrible, which was really not how I felt at all, even though my stomach did this little lurch.

"And I can see you think this is a lousy idea, so just forget I even brought it up. I was just—"

"Hey, hey, hey—gimme a sec here."

He went and stood over by the window, looking out, though you can really only see tree branches and pieces of sky 'cause there's these two giant sycamores right in front of the window.

"I guess," I said after a minute, "I always figured we'd get married. We always talk like we will but I just thought we'd wait until both of us were done with school. Your training was only two years but I have three more years to go and so I figured after that—"

"You figured we'd wait three more years?"

"I guess. I don't know. I don't think I really thought it out all that specifically. I just figured, you know, sometime around then." There was this awful silence that I knew meant that was definitely the wrong answer. "Come sit over here."

"I'm fine where I am, thanks."

And I made sure not to let him see me smile, 'cause that was exactly how he got when he was hurt, all "No big deal to me one way or the other, I'm just fine" kind of attitude. I got up out of bed, came up behind him and squeezed myself between him and the window, wrapping my arms around his neck.

"Hey, I would love to marry you, and you know that. You know how crazy I am about you and I'm always talking about those five kids I want, and how I want to save for one of those houses on Bay Farm Island, on the lagoons. Remember at Stacy's wedding I was saying how I think the Venetian Hour is so pretentious—"

"Five kids is a lot, May."

"You think?"

"Yeah. I mean three or four is plenty."

"Yeah, maybe."

"I don't want to wait three years, May."

"Okay. Okay. Maybe that's a long time—"

"Shit, May, we've been going out for five years."

"Yeah, I know. And I want to. Just not right now."

"Don't be doing me any big favors, May."

"Don't get like that. Can we talk about it again in a year?"

"Sure. Whatever."

"Sure, whatever," I said, imitating him.

"Shut up, all right?" He pulled away from me, sat over on the bed and ran his hands through his hair, shaking his head. "Shit."

"What?"

"That was harder than I thought. I think next year you should do it."

"What? Propose?"

"Yeah, you're such the big Nineties feminist career woman, you propose next time."

"I think I could do a better job."

"Oh, yeah?"

"Ah, *yeah*—ah, ah, well, I was thinking, miss," I said in a Gomer Pile voice, "maybe we can go get hitched and—"

"Oh, you're dead." And he grabbed me, covering my mouth, but I was laughing so hard I had to pull his hand away so I could breathe. When we kissed I was thinking the whole time how lucky I was to have Buddy, could see him at the end of some aisle, looking all cramped and fidgety in a tuxedo.

The next time he proposed I put him off again but by the third time it was Christmas of my junior year and he had an actual ring.

"Jesus, May, people go to school when they're married. There's no rule that says you can't be married and go to college, for Christ's sake." And besides, we'd set a date for the following February so I'd only have one more semester anyway.

But then the accident happened. He never did ask for the ring back, and the way it ended with me storming out and him going to Mexico, I never got the chance to try to give it back. I keep it in its little red velvet box in my jewelry box, since I don't have much jewelry and don't have to hardly look in there anyway. The wedding was going to be in Buddy's backyard. They have this huge yard with all of Angela's roses lining the fence and a gazebo that Joe made mostly for the wedding. And the other stuff, the caterer, the cake, Kate canceled for me. I never got a chance to order any flowers.

I know he's been home. They're a tight family and he wouldn't be gone for three years and not come home for a visit. Christmas, in particular, is a huge deal for Buddy's family and so it hurts more because I know he can't have had second thoughts. I'd have heard from him.

I got up out of bed then, pulled on a robe and went in the kitchen to make coffee. I'm an idiot, but while the coffee's brewing, I rummaged around in the bottom bookshelf where I keep the photo albums. I should just throw them out, but I have this one picture of Buddy that kills me every time I see it. It's from one Fourth of July when he had to work and came by with the actual fire truck and all these guys on their way home from a fire, Randy ringing the bell, and Joe was loving it, throwing like twenty burgers on the grill, and Angela was running in the house to put more beers in the cooler and I yelled, "Buddy!" and when he looked over, all grimy and smiling, I took it. He looks so happy, like the happiest guy you've ever seen. It kills me.

Chapter 10

I stay in touch with Jack. Once every couple weeks or so one of us picks up the phone to say hi.

"I got a postcard from Kate," he said last week when he called, "from a place called Southampton."

"A windmill?" I asked.

"What?"

"The postcard, does it have a windmill on it?"

"No, a beach."

"Yeah," I told him, "there's a lot of beaches on Long Island. You should check out a map."

"I did."

"So, what did it say?" I asked, pouring myself a Diet Coke in a glass, watching it fizz over the ice cubes.

"Here, I'll read it; 'Dear Jack, I just wanted you to know that I am fine. I hope one day you can understand and forgive me. Love, Kate.' What the hell is that supposed to mean? 'Understand and forgive' what?"

I sat at the kitchen table, put my feet up on another chair and looked at my postcard I have stuck to the side of the refrigerator. "I guess that she's left."

"But how can I understand and forgive if I don't know why she left? I mean, why couldn't she just say to me, 'Jack, I need to leave you to go to Southampton'? I mean, what choice would I have had?"

I smiled. "Oh, Jack, that's much too practical for Kate. Not nearly enough excitement in that." I laughed a little, a commiserative kind of laugh Jack and I do with each other. Whatever misgivings I'd had about Jack before Kate left have melted away in the months she's been gone. We've become these sad little war widows, sighing, clicking our tongues, reaching across a table at Java Rama to squeeze each other's hands.

"It's been over four months, May. Do you think she's coming back?"

"I don't know. I hope so." This is another thing we do for each other. One of us asks the question we are both thinking and the other reassures without promising, but that day I was feeling different, tired and weary of this waiting and so I added, "But she might not, Jack. You need to consider that. And really, do you want a relationship with someone who can just disappear on you one day?" I flinched as I said this because I realized that really, or maybe just also, I was talking about Buddy and that Jack, who got to hear the whole story over too many lattés at Java Rama one afternoon, would know it too.

But kindly, gently, he just said, "But I love her, May."

"I know, but it's not good for you to just wait around for her like this. You should get out more. Let Will fix you up with that girl from Oracle."

"Oh, May, I'm not ready for that."

"So, go anyway. It's just a date. You don't have to marry her, for God's sake."

"Look who's talking, Miss One Date a Decade herself. Why don't you follow some of your own advice?"

"I am."

"You're dating someone?"

"You don't have to say it like that, like it's some sort of miracle or something"

"You're joking. How long you've been dating this guy?"

"Scott. His name is Scott. About a month."

"A month! And you haven't said anything? Well, that's great. That's great, May. So, you've gotta tell me about him. So, you're, like, getting' some then, right? You are getting some, aren't you?"

"I don't really think—"

"Don't give me that, May."

"Yeah," I said. "Sure."

"Like, how much?"

"Jesus, Jack!"

"I'm just happy for you, May. I just want to know *how* happy for you I should be."

"I'm hanging up, Jack."

"Oh, come on, May. Let me live vicariously through you."

"I'm saying good-bye, Jack."

"So, is it everything you remembered?"

"'Bye Jack." I hung up, smiling, shaking my head. I put my glass in the dishwasher. The truth is, I think, things could get serious with Scott. Betsy's invited him over for Thanksgiving and he's bringing his daughter, Morgan, to meet me for the first time, as this is his holiday with her. Something about the idea of meeting Morgan makes me feel a little sweaty, like I'm going on some job interview. But it's become more than a series of dates, and I even talk to him about Kate.

My missing Kate has become its own thing, like some little plant I watch over, picking off the brown leaves, misting it, watching it grow in ways I can't predict. It grows all weedy and wild. First it was this desperate, frantic feeling, and then anger that swiped me from behind, and now it's settled in the back of my throat, a dull tender aching. I have this suspicion that Kate really may not come back, that something has happened inside her that we cannot know, and that even if she does come back, nothing will be the same. I don't say this to Jack. It would break his heart. When I've said this to Betsy she's nodded, but says, "Maybe, and maybe she's just upping the ante."

For Thanksgiving, I made my pecan cornbread stuffing and wore my burgundy velour dress, the one with the half-sleeves that's cool enough to cook in. I also made Kate's stuffed artichokes, a recipe she learned in junior-high home ec. My gaze went from the cutting board to the stained and faded ditto as I chopping parsley, measured oil, spooned stuffing between the leaves, and I thought I might lose it, right in the kitchen with Betsy stirring cranberries on the stove, my face moist with the steam of mulled cider. I don't even like artichokes. They taste like eating houseplants, stuffing or no stuffing.

I shoved the rest of the stuffing in the artichokes, washed my hands and told Betsy, "I'll get some soda from the garage."

"May?"

I swung around like some caged animal but she just handed me a mug of cider and turned back to her cranberries. It was times like this that I loved Betsy, the way she really didn't need to talk about it and could leave you alone. I hit the garage door opener and ducked under the door as it was still opening. It was cold outside, for Alameda, and I walked slowly to the end of the driveway and peered down the street. Some family, a block down, was climbing out of their Highlander, unloading aluminum-foil-covered pans from the trunk. A little kid dragged his stuffed monkey along the ground. Henry had started a fire in the living room, and between the smell and the monkey bouncing along the street that's *it* for me. I headed back up the driveway lined with the graying hydrangea and browning grass, colors blurry through my tears, and I was just hating Kate. Thanksgiving was the first holiday after our mother killed herself and it was an actual unwritten rule that you are at home for Thanksgiving. But that's the thing about Kate. She's just selfish and thoughtless enough not to remember that, to think that whatever drama is going on with her gives her a waiver from what has been the rule all these years.

"Can you grab a couple of these chairs?"

Startled, I looked up to see Henry standing in the garage, a wooden folding chair under each arm.

"Sure," I said. The chairs were filmed with grime from sitting in the garage and Henry wiped two down with a rag and handed them to me. Then he looked at me, at my wet lashes and blotchy face. "It's a hard day," I said in response. "You know, Kate, Mom."

He nodded. "Yeah, me too. I kept thinking, as you girls got older, that I'd forget what it was like that first Thanksgiving without your mom. The way the two of you were—anyway, I don't."

"How *were* we?"

He sighed, leaned the chairs he was holding back up against the garage wall and glanced out onto the street. "Dazed. You kind of wandered around your grandma's house like you were lost, and Kate went from the dining room table to the couch, just staring at the Macy's Day Parade on TV. We had the TV on the whole day 'cause it just felt like there was too much silence. And then, you know your mother hated the TV so having it on just made things even stranger."

I sort of remembered, in the wispy ways of dreams. I was wandering because I was looking for my coloring book, the one the nurse had given me, and when I found it I sat on the living room floor, as near to Kate as I dared, and colored each page, one after the other, leaning on the coffee table, sharpening the soft silver and copper and gold that wear down so fast.

"But she loved books," I said, "and drawing."

"And she loved shopping," Henry added, and we smiled, the deep smiles of memory. This was the little ritual we would do when I was a kid, reciting, "the things Mommy loved," a way for me not to forget her. "And she was beautiful," he said, the same way he had forever, urgent and wistful, so I always could see, no matter what else was confusing me in my life at the time, that he loved her.

Henry reached over and we hugged tight till I was finally ready to pull away. "Thanks. I'm okay now."

Ten minutes later, as Betsy and I stood, bent over, staring at the turkey thermometer, watching the thin red line rise, the doorbell rang.

"It's Jamie and Rich," Henry called from the front door.

"The heck with them," I called back. "Where's that baby?"

"Ah, *that* was it," Rich says, thumping his head. "I told you we were forgetting something," he said to Jamie.

"We're going to call him Charles," Jamie said as I scooped the baby from his arms.

"Come here, sweetie," I cooed. "Come to Auntie May."

"He didn't come with a name?" Henry asked as we made our way into the living room.

"Archie," Rich said.

"Ah, I see. That's very kind of you then."

They only stayed for a half-hour on their way to Jamie's mother's house, but I got to change Charles's tiny little diaper and try to feed him a bottle he wasn't really in the mood for.

As we stood out in the driveway, Jamie buckling Charles into his car seat, Rich said, "So, honey, we just wanted to come by, give you a hug. With Kate being gone and all we know—" He wrapped his big arms around me.

"I'm not going to cry again," I said, but of course I did.

I watched them pull out of the driveway and disappear around the corner, then went back into the house, wondering just what Kate could be doing and thinking today, if maybe she was crying a little bit too.

"Do I take my shoes off?" Morgan asked in this thick marbley voice. I saw my share of seven-year-olds at the library and she was clearly tall for her age, with these big loppy orange curls Scott had pulled to the side with a blue bow.

"The shoes," Scott said, pointing to her shoes. They were actual red glitter Mary Janes, a la *The Wizard of Oz.*

"Ohhh. I see. Are those new?" I asked.

She nodded, beaming.

"Don't take them off. Never take them off," I whispered, leading her to the table.

"Why?"

I shook my head in mock disbelief. "It's a long story. Witch, heirloom shoes, farm girl," I told her. "I'll fill you in later."

The meal was an odd mixture of forced manners and uneasiness. It was so strange for Kate to not be passing her artichokes and loading the dishwasher. Morgan sat between me and Scott. Scott cut her turkey and green beans into tiny pieces, which she pushed around her plate. She asked for more mashed potatoes, spilled a dollop of it on the lap of her navy velvet dress and gasped.

"Come on," I said. "If we clean that right now it might not stain." I got out of my chair and extended my hand.

She considered my offer for a moment and then hopped from her chair, sliding a warm soft hand into mine.

"This is such a pretty dress." I crouched down in front of her, wiping the spot with the wet end of a dishtowel. "I think this will help." She looked skeptical; the white spot seemed to be spreading. I switched to blotting and that seemed to help.

"Are you my father's girlfriend?" she asked. I stopped blotting to meet her gaze, an expression that if it didn't mean so much business would be comical.

"Well, I wouldn't say 'girlfriend.' Friend. We're friends."

"I thought you were dating."

"Who told you that?"

"He did. And my mother."

"Oh. Well, yes, that's true." I stood up. I was starting to feel like I needed the height advantage and I'd done about all I could with the spot.

"Well, then why'd you lie?"

"I didn't lie."

"You said you weren't his girlfriend."

"That's only because when you get to be my age you don't really use that particular word."

She raised her eyebrows at me like she'd heard that one before. "Am I coming here for Christmas?"

"What? No. No, I don't think so."

She just nodded, looking all serene with that bit of information.

Suddenly I was all agitated. "Come on. Our food is probably ice cold."

"Your dress is pretty too."

I swung around and caught her smiling at me. She reached out to finger my skirt.

"Thanks."

When we were done, Henry took Morgan up to Kate's old room to look for her old Barbie case with the Crewcut Barbie, Measles Barbie, Tattoo Skipper and Anatomically Incorrect Ken—and Scott and I went out for a walk.

"You know, May, you have an awful nice family."

"Why do you say that?'

"I don't know. I just noticed. When Gail and I were still together for the holidays, especially the last few years, it was always kind of tense. Even if we didn't have a fight, it was like something was right there, underneath the surface. And Gail and my mother didn't really hit it off, so if we were there for the holiday it was the same tenseness but with me feeling like the referee."

"What about her family?"

"They're actually very nice. Hal, her dad, is one of those quiet, dutiful types, the right balance of easygoingness and control. I guess the kind of guy I wanted my father to be."

"Why? What kind of guy was your father?"

"The kind that leaves when you're six and shows up occasionally with some toy you're too old for. He's out of the picture now."

"Oh. I'm sorry."

"Yeah. It was tough, but at least it taught me who I didn't want to be. That's why this separation is so tough. I didn't want to do the same thing to my own kid."

"Well, it hardly seems the same to me. I mean—"

"I know. I know. I'm very involved and Gail and I don't backstab each other to Morgan. I pay my child support. But you know it doesn't make up for not being in the house every night, at the dinner table, when she goes to bed. I know what that feels like."

"What happened between you and Gail?"

"Oh, you know how it is, May. You ask us both and we'll give you different answers. I think Gail asked me to leave because I'm not her father, you know. I'm a teacher, so money's always tight and she's not used to that. Her father made plenty and her mother stayed home, and as much as Gail said she was going back to Aetna when Morgan was a year old she felt forced, not ready, when the time came, and she resented me for it. I think that's what made it possible to have the affair."

"She had an affair?"

"Yeah, her parents kept up her membership at the tennis club, and he was some guy she knew from there, grew up with really. Hey, you don't want to be hearing all this, do you? Shit. I'm just going on and on."

"No. I'm not feeling that way. I feel like you know all this stuff about me from Betsy and I hardly know anything about you. Anyway, so what would Gail say?"

"What? Oh, you mean about the separation? Well, I think she would just say I wasn't as interesting to her anymore."

"That's harsh."

He shrugged, like maybe he thought it was true. We walked all the way down Grand to where it dead-ends into the beach.

I led us over to a bench and we sat down, just quiet, with the sound of the wind and the waves in my ears. Scott took my hand, kissed me.

When we got back to the house Jack's Prelude was in the driveway.

"May, look who'd here," Betsy called as we came inside.

They were sitting at the cleared dining room table, passing cream and sugar, stirring coffee.

"Don't get up. Betsy I can get ours." I leaned over the back of Jack's chair to kiss him on the cheek. "Happy Thanksgiving."

He stood up to shake Scott's hand and I heard him say, "Caught yourself one beauty with May here."

I whirled around to mouth "shut up," which he loved, a little gleam in his eye, but he changed the subject.

Coming back to the table with our coffee I heard the sirens on the TV. Betsy stopped too, a plate of pumpkin pie in her hand, and I stared at the TV, transfixed, as the firemen ran shouting back and forth behind the news anchor.

"I'm here at the Alameda Naval Air Station where at approximately three fifteen this afternoon a fire was reported in the naval station commissary. The commissary itself has been shut down for some time now, but it has been reported that several homeless people might be living inside the building. The Alameda fire department has been on the scene since three thirty and believe they should have the fire under control in the next hour. Back to you, John."

I switched off the remote. When I turned Scott was looking at me, confused.

"Oh, sorry," I mumbled. "Here's your coffee."

Jack caught my eye and beckoned me to the chair next to Scott.

"Pumpkin or pecan," I heard Betsy say.

"Pecan," I said, leaning back in my chair.

Chapter 11

It was two weeks before Christmas when Jack called to tell me he was moving in with his friend Will, that "Thanksgiving was it," the too-painful night that made him have to admit that even if Kate was coming back things would be too messy and confusing. There'd be too many words and feelings for two people in those four rooms.

"And I know I can't face Christmas," he said. "I see myself walking through that front door Christmas Eve, waking up here Christmas morning, and I'm telling you, May, I can't do it."

So I drove to the apartment after work, six empty Safeway produce boxes in the backseat and trunk. Jack was still at work as I made my trips from the dark parking lot into the apartment. I turned on all the lights, wandering from room to room, gazing at every surface for a sign of Kate. And truthfully—poor Jack—they were everywhere. Her sewing machine sat in the corner of the living room with pieces of a blouse she was working on, pale melon cotton pinned with the waxed pattern paper in a sloppy stack on the little machine table. I flipped open the old cigar boxes my grandmother had given her, filled with spools of thread, then let the lids fall closed and went into the galley kitchen.

Jack was either neater than I thought or he had cleaned up for me. The kitchen smelled of Ajax, the gritty film sticking to my finger as I ran it along the sink bottom, and one coffee cup sat upside down in the dish rack. The old breadbox Kate picked up at a garage sale was empty. A note from Jack on the counter said he had finally washed and folded the clothes that were in her hamper. I could picture him, lifting the pile to his face to inhale her smell as he carried it to the laundry room.

After my mother died, on one of our first trips back to the house, I pulled a cool, crumpled T-shirt out of my parents' hamper, checked it for her scent and carried it into the car with me. I saw my father glance at it in my lap and panicked for a second that he would take it from me, but he didn't. He merely sighed softly to himself, started the car and pulled out of the driveway. I keep the T-shirt stuffed in the back of my underwear drawer, and while it's taken on the scent of the different sachets I keep in there, I still tell myself, all these years later, that I remember her smell and it's on there. So, I knew how Jack was letting go of Kate, one uncurled finger at a time.

The clothes sat, as the note said, folded on the bed. I plopped down next to them, across from the door to Kate's closet, and in that moment I felt how I've been dreading this, how packing Kate up in produce boxes is about as close to saying good-bye as you can get. I could see Henry, Betsy and me carrying the boxes up to Kate's room, stacking them in a corner for the cleaning woman to dust off when she comes each week.

"Jesus, Kate," I said aloud, "you've really done it this time."

I opened the closet and realized I'd need many more boxes than I'd brought and something about having to come back was a relief.

I emptied her dresser, then her nightstand, filled all but the last box. I slid my hand between the mattress and box spring and found her journal. It was where she always kept it and as I paged through to the last entry I wondered why I hadn't thought of this before, to look for a hint here.

~

7-18-

It's pretty certain I'll be teaching the curtain class in September. Finally. I told Lois I could do it. I know it's the new medicine helping me get out of bed and to work on time but I'm taking some of the credit too. I told Dr. Eliot I've been wanting to do this and I've been (as he says) keeping my eye on the ball. Jack is working again tonight, which is just as well since I'm feeling sick. I'm going to bed early—don't want to miss a day of work now.

And that was it. Two days later they had the fight and the day after that was when Jack called me. I flipped through the rest of the journal but there was nothing, really, and I put the journal at the bottom of the last box. I carried armload after armload, seven trips, of hanging clothes from the closet to the backseat of my car. They spilled onto the floor, getting all wrinkled, but I didn't care. She deserved worse than wrinkled clothes for making me do this. With the clothes gone I could see two cardboard boxes, one on top of the other, pushed up against the back of the closet; a pile of shoes and boots; and a plastic laundry basket of purses. I should have asked Betsy to help me. I crawled into the closet and started throwing the shoes out the door, making a pile next to the bed. I stood up to lift the top box out.

"Ow!"

Something had poked me hard in the back. It was too cramped to turn around but I reached my hand back and felt a metal coat hook and then rubbed the spot on my back as the pain faded.

"Jesus Christ." I'd had it. I told myself I'd done enough for one night. I would just pull these two boxes out and come back tomorrow after work—with help.

The top box was heavy and I dropped it to the floor, pushed it out of the closet and then pushed the bottom one out too. I crawled out of the closet, all huffing, puffing, sweaty, and sat up against the side of the bed to catch my breath.

How do I get these jobs? This was so typical—me cleaning up Kate's mess, literally. I looked over at one of the boxes. It had *JOURNALS* written in black marker along the side. I opened the top and sure enough, there they were, some twenty years of Kate's diaries. Four stacks inside the box and I reached down to the bottom of a stack and pulled one out. It was small and pink with a lock, the type Kate liked in elementary school and junior high, before she moved on to the bigger, booklike ones without the locks. The little key on pink embroidery thread was in the lock and I turned it, heard its tinny spring pop open with a sound so familiar I smiled, remembering all the times I snuck in her room to read her diaries. I was always secretly disappointed she didn't write about me.

I put the journal back in the box, closed it up and opened the other box. It was the smell, musty and strange, that stopped me. Inside the box lay a journal, red with the remnants of gold lettering *DIARY* on its cover, and three dresses, identical, in pale green, baby blue and yellow. I pushed the little gold button to unlock the diary and it popped open. I opened to the middle and in that instant, the instant I saw the loopy script, the high Ts and Is, I realized these were not Kate's letters. I put the book up to my face, inhaling the smell, and I knew, in a way that has no words, that this was something else. I knew because that little boy's face flashed in front in my mind and when I flipped to the front page I was right.

This Diary Belongs to Liza Small.

I unfolded each dress and lay them in a row on the bed and for a moment I just stared at them, trying to imagine my mother wearing them. I took the blue one and held it up to my face, inhaled the musty smell. The journal was dated 35 years earlier. I began to read.

2-4-72

Dr. Lane was late himself this morning so I couldn't help but say, "What do you think this may mean?" arching my eyebrows the way he does.

He looked all caught and pleased at the same time and said, "I suppose it means I got a flat on the way over here."

"Oh, really?" I never would have gotten away with that kind of excuse. I know. I tried that actual one with the last therapist I had. Honestly, though, I could tell he was being truthful. His knees were all greasy and dirty and he even had a smear of it on his neck. Still, I'm surprised he answered me instead of asking me what it means to me that he was late. Maybe I should just be my

own shrink. Set up two chairs and alternately cry and nod at myself and then take the fifty dollars and buy that adorable purse I saw in Nordstrom's.

Anyway, rain, rain, rain all day today and yesterday and looks like tomorrow and I could scream. I hate when my feet are cold.

After my session I stopped by the library for the most boring book on earth for my literature essay on Keats and it's a tome of a thing—practically needed its own little wagon to haul it back home. Luckily Rachel came over today to study. We've got the worst English assignment: "What's the most difficult thing you've ever done?" Honestly! Why in the world would I ever share such a thing with a teacher. I'll have to lie. I hate to lie. But it looks like I'll have to as it is due tomorrow.

I can't tell you how long I sat there, but when I looked up at the nightstand clock it was almost eleven and I needed to leave. Jack would be home at any minute and I didn't want to see him, to see anyone, right now. With the two boxes in the front seat beside me, I pulled out of the parking lot, the soft swish of the windshield wipers going. And it was the windshield wipers, the warm defroster and the memory of her voice that wrapped themselves around me like sitting in her car, right before she drove off the dock. And I felt like I was stepping into a dark, dark hole, scared but unable to stop, so I kept walking. My mind was racing. Where did the box come from? Why did Kate have it? How could she not tell me? And why would she leave them?

I carried each box into my bedroom, dropped them on my bed. I climbed into bed with the boxes beside me, as if someone would steal them, like Kate and my mother were sleeping in those boxes. I knew as I switched off the lamp that I wouldn't sleep, that too many pictures were swirling inside me, too many questions and the same question over and over again: Was the reason my mother drove us into the bay hidden in that journal?

But I was wrong. I did sleep, thickly, solidly, and when I awoke, the boxes were still there, not a dream. I stretched and reached for the red one. I stood, reading it in the kitchen, with the sound of the coffee dripping in its pot.

2-12-72

Accepted to Bryn Mawr! Letter came in the mail today. Mother said straight out, "Well, my dear, looks like we'll have to get you a winter coat. It gets terribly cold in Pennsylvania in the winter." Despite all her reservations I could tell she was pleased for me—either that or Daddy won. I could hardly believe it. I ran down the hall to call Rachel and then we were both screaming and jumping up and down on the phone until we remembered that she was not going to Bryn Mawr. In fact, she may not be going to college at all if that Eddie Jackson proposes like she thinks he will. So then we both burst into tears because either way we'll be entirely too far away, but then I, or maybe it was Rachel, decided that we would just fly back and forth, that that would be perfect, spending time together, shopping, going out to lunch and seeing movies, staying up all night without some parent telling us what movies are and are not appropriate for young ladies. Oh, and of course, if we have homework we can do that too.

I'm going to be a teacher, I think. I know I said lawyer but the other day I saw a class of elementary school children on a field trip with handmade name tags hanging from their necks by yarn. A smiling young woman with lovely skin was leading them down the street like little ducklings. Oh, can hardly believe this. I must call Dr. Lane.

I left a message with his service. I hung up and got this fluttering feeling in my chest. I'll miss Dr. Lane. He's helped me with my episodes and he believes in me, that I can be a teacher or a lawyer. Even last summer when I said I wanted to work at the zoo, he just nodded like it was the most normal thing in the world. When I came back from my visit at the zoo to say it was too smelly of a job, he just nodded some more. That's what a wonderful doctor he is—to suggest I explore the option thoroughly, as he says, before leaping. He's always saying that. "Look before you leap, Liza." He says it over and over again but I like to hear it—all those L's. But I do think I'm on to something with being a teacher.

2-13-72

Almost done with my valentines. I bought this lovely shiny red and pink paper. I'm going to send it as a secret admirer valentine to Johnny Ray. To-

night, after Mother and Father go to sleep I'm going to sneak out and put it in his mailbox. He's three blocks down the street and I should be there and back in no time.

Carol Bisk is going to Bryn Mawr also. She is a bit full of herself, or shy. It's hard to tell, but she doesn't usually go to parties or come shopping, and I don't believe she's had more than a couple boyfriends and she may be poor. Also, her father is an archeologist at UCLA and they whisk her out of school for months at a time to go to places like Kenya and Africa—or is Kenya in Africa? I'll have to look that up in the atlas. If we're going to be friends I don't want to make a complete fool of myself. I think I'll call her right now and see if she wants to be roommates. Carol is very tall, probably 5'9", and has stick-straight blond hair, almost like straw, and is pale, pale, pale, even her eyes are pale blue, like she ever so narrowly escaped being albino, and her voice is soft so that she hardly seems to be there at all, like she might go all shimmery and step through a wall. Still, better quiet Carol for a roommate than some stranger. Girls come from all over to Bryn Mawr and I could end up with some New Yorker.

Hate quiet Carol. Full of herself. She already has a roommate, some girl she met in Nigeria.

"We can still spend lots of time together," she told me, like she was letting me down easy. That only made me more angry. It's not that I need her as a friend. It just would have been convenient is all.

Rachel and I are going to Coronado Island with our families for Easter break. We planned this months ago, to get our parents to vacation in the same place, so we could go off together and not get stuck with our parents or poor Rachel with that horrid brother of hers, Marcus. Date with James Powell tonight. We're going to see Oklahoma.

2-19-72

I think I'm in love with James. I think I definitely am. And to think I almost didn't let him take me out because I had my eye on Johnny Ray. Good thing it was raining the night before Valentine Day so I couldn't leave the valentine. I just gave it to Rachel. On the way to see Butterflies Are Free, *while we were waiting for the light to change, I looked over at James and realized what absolutely gorgeous eyes he has, deep brown. His nose and chin are a little sharp but his hair is a thick rich brown. He wants to be a veterinarian. I love animals and so yet another reason why we are meant to be. I know this is true love and I can tell by the way he looks at me that he thinks so too, although a boy wouldn't ever say such a thing. I guess I will have to cancel my date with Johnny for next weekend because we're sure to be going steady by then. I should go do that right now.*

Done. He took it quite well, even though I could tell he didn't believe I might have the whooping cough. He really is a nice boy.

2-20-72

James called me right after church to see if I wanted to go get an ice cream. It's a bit cold for an ice cream and there's no way I'll fit into my gray dress if I eat anything—never a mind an ice cream—this week. But not to worry. I'll just drop it.

7 p.m. Kissed me right on the sidewalk on the way back from ice cream. Thought I would melt right into the pavement and then panicked, worrying Mrs. Braxton would be peering through her drapes at us and call my mother, but I didn't see her. Oh, God—must call Rachel and tell her. We can both be married this spring. We could have a double wedding! Oh yes, that's perfect. Then we can live next door to each other and our children can play together. Oh, there's the phone!

I thought maybe that was Rachel—or James missing me and wanting to talk—but it was the evil Mrs. Braxton. Seems she was peering through the upstairs curtains. She and Mother play bridge together so she feels it's her obligation to keep Mother posted on such disgraceful behavior. Endured fifteen minutes of lecture at the kitchen table about appearances, nice girls and the importance of taking my medication. Daddy came in at one point from the garden to wash his hands and winked at me behind her back. I wish I only had Father, and Mother could meet with some terrible accident—maybe something particularly tragic so that we would be in the paper. Anyways, I feel fine and don't need to be taking my medication right now. It makes me feel thick and drowsy and that's the last thing a girl needs when she is about to be engaged.

Feeling much better without stupid medicine. Much more energy and plenty of mental health. Dr. Lane doesn't suspect a thing because I'm right. I don't need the medication and he and Mother will see I'm right and anyway when I'm married I won't be accountable to either of them.

2-23-72
Luckily not very hungry at all so hardly eating and becoming lovely swan-like, ballerina-type beauty. James and I are going to dinner and for a drive Friday night. He calls me every night. He is smitten.

2-25-72
Dr. Lane suspects something. He is asking me about my medication but I was able to look him straight in the face and tell him I take every dose—just as he prescribed. Still, I don't think he believed me and may call Mother. If he does that I know she'll make me stay home tonight and then I will have to die. I know. I'll disconnect the phone. By the time they notice I will be gone.

2-25-72 11 p.m.
Oh, dear. Had some bourbon James had in his car made me feel so nice at first but then so sleepy then we started kissing couldn't stop I can't even write it down—too much. Maybe a dream. Oh, dear. Must be a dream because James is too nice of a guy and I'm too nice of a girl—late. Will go to sleep and hopefully awake with more clarity.

2-26-72
Oh, God! Did awake with more clarity and am terrified. What have I done?! I need to call Rachel.

Rachel is right. When you are in love and destined to be together losing one's virginity is incidental. Not feeling so well. Think I'll take a dose or two of my medication since I don't need to fit into the gray dress anymore.

Not feeling so well. Staying in bed today.

2-28-72

Feeling much better today but have gym class and hate gym and the ugly blue-snapped gym uniform, so made believe I'm still sick. Told James I was staying home, so he called after school to see how I was doing. His family has a weekend house in La Jolla and we're going to sneak down there on Saturday night. James made a copy of the key. His father writes screenplays and his mother used to be a model—clearly she has passed on her genes to her son.

Saw Dr. Lane today. He never did call Mother and all is fine because I feel perfect in every way. Love is the best medicine. Who needs pills?

3-5-72

Too busy and madly in love to write. Virginity is vastly overrated—especially when you are planning to be married anyway. Tonight, while we were lying in his bed in his La Jolla room—which romantically looks out over the water—James told me he is going to UCLA and that that being the case I certainly can't go to Bryn Mawr. I knew it!! And then he said, "I don't ever want to be away from you."

He'll propose any day now. I just know it.

3-7-72

Oh, can't sleep a wink—too excited—need to pick dress flowers bridesmaids. Might as well get dressed since can't sleep and want to go to Italy to get lace and beading for dress, need to find out about flights to Italy and where most wonderful seamstress in Rome is for dress. Maybe glass slippers and a big long train and then will make guest list—Rachel Mary Lisa Johnny Jeff—maybe Mother Father and all boring aunts and uncles including bad-smelling Uncle Reed. Off I go to the airport.

3-15-72

In hospital. Locked ward. Had another episode and climbed up on our roof this time to see the stars. Was not planning to jump or anything just wanted to see the stars and knew that with enough moonlight and crickets could easily fly like an airplane—or at least float to the ground—but I honestly wasn't planning to try. Finally, today, I got Father to bring me my dairy. He handed it to me and I slid it under my pillow while Mother was in the bathroom. Couldn't trust her not to read it. She did bring me a decent nightgown though. Oh dear, must sleep, very groggy from horrid new medicine and cannot cheek it because nurse is two hundred years old and knows all tricks and sticks disgusting finger in my mouth if she suspects I am. No phone to call James. Must call and fib about where I am.

3-18-72

Mother said James called today and she told him I was in bed too ill to talk. He called Rachel and, clever girl that she is she figured it right out and went on to tell him how I am such a fragile flower that I occasionally need to take to the bed to regain my strength. She said he was concerned but understood I would be well soon. Love Rachel for the wonderful friend that she is. She also agrees that he will propose any day.

4-1-72

Home now but dear God, I think I am pregnant. I told Dr. Lane yesterday and he drew blood right then and there. I was so afraid to tell him but I didn't know what else to do. He even promised not to tell my mother a thing—yet. He said "yet" as we don't know if there is anything to worry about. Dr. Lane thought I was joking with him at first. I haven't told anyone. I need to call Rachel. P.S. NOT horrid April Fool's joke.

4-2-72

I told Rachel last night and dear friend that she is she cried for me. That finally made me cry. I threw up this morning—it's Easter—but it may be from nerves. Rachel says I should tell James and that he will have to marry me right away—that he will, of course, want to marry me since he loves me. I need to be sure first. Maybe I'm wrong.

4-3-72

2 a.m.—can't sleep. I got up and called Dr. Lane and his service got him at his house. He's going to see me first thing tomorrow morning. He says we should have the results by then. He said I can take another sleeping pill so I did but not feeling drowsy at all.

4-4-72

This is my last entry. I will kill myself tonight, after my parents fall asleep. Dr. Lane called my parents and told them. Before I could even tell James my father called his father and they have told us we are forbidden to see each other. I flew into such a rage I threw my father's ashtray across the room. It smashed on the floor with cigarette butts everywhere, which you know just pushed Mother to the brink. He didn't say a word but slapped me hard across the face. Mother actually gasped but you know she approved. She was just shocked. She is so hateful and mean. I know how pleased it made her to have Daddy lose his temper with me. It took every ounce of strength I had to hold back the tears. Then they sent me to my room and closed the door to the study. I ran to the phone and called James but his mother answered so I hung up. I'm glad I threw the stupid ashtray. I'd do it again, I would, if I got the chance.

4-19-72

No abortion. Mother made that perfectly clear when Dr. Lane broached the subject this morning. As if she wasn't mortified enough. I thought she was going to hit him for even bringing it up. I leave Thursday morning and go directly to the airport to fly to Pennsylvania, where I will stay until I have the baby. Pennsylvania!!! I tried to talk Mother out of it. It's so far—and cold! But she just threw the rosaries on my bed, so I knew. She had been to see Father Thomas, which must have required a strong bourbon afterward. All she would say was, "Father Thomas had another girl, years ago, that he sent there." She emphasized "years ago" like a sin this awful hardly ever happens. Rachel came to visit me one day in the hospital and brought a letter from James. He does still love me and knows from Rachel that my parents are sending me to Pennsylvania to have the baby. I know it's his parents who won't let him marry me, but he wants to and as soon as he turns eighteen this June he will drive out to get me and we'll be married. I would give anything to speak to him. I am so woozy from the medicine and my mouth feels like it's full of cotton, but I don't care. I'm so nauseous. I feel not quite myself, like a hundred broken pieces that have been swept up off the floor and glued together every which way. I cannot bear to be away from James. I will wait until later and then sneak up to his room in the middle of the night and we will run away together.

4-21-72

The Powells have an alarm system that went off the minute I broke the window. Even though I ran away they knew it was me, and Mother, Father and the police were waiting for me when I got home. I screamed and yelled so loud that the stupid policeman just stood there like he didn't know what to do. Idiot. Mother grabbed me and practically threw me in the house, but I kept right on screaming—all the way to the hospital. I do feel better here. My body feels less cold and trembly and somehow it's more comfortable to be groggy and cotton-mouthed on the unit—and they gave me my same room.

Father came to visit me last night and pulled a chair right up to my bed. When I first came to the hospital last week Father walked into the room and yelled so loud the doctor came and took him away saying, "Come on now. That won't do any good." Father shrugged him off, but when he came back in the room he was calmer and that's when he told me about how I was going to this home for unwed mothers, someplace run by nuns, and how Marlborough School thinks I am going for my emotional problems so no one will be the wiser when I get back. He said it all like I should be happy. But what does he know about being in love? He's married to Mother. So, tonight he pulled a bag of double-salted licorice that I love out of his pocket and handed it to me and then said, "Liza, I don't know what to do with you. I hope you will take this time away to reflect on your life and choose a different path."

"There is no different path," I told him. "I'm in love with James and I will marry him."

"Liza," he said, "James does not want to marry you."

Liar! He is a liar. He just told me that because he does what Mother tells him to do. Still, I don't know why James hasn't tried to sneak in to see me. If he was in here I would have figured a way to sneak in and see him. I would have dressed up as a nurse or a candy striper. Nothing would have kept me away. I'm sure of it. Maybe he will come this week before I leave. Oh, God, think I'm going to throw up!

Chapter 12

I was late. I showered like a madwoman, shoved a Lean Cuisine into my purse, grabbed the journal and was out the door.

I want to ditch work and go sit somewhere where I can keep reading and drink some very strong coffee, but I can't. We're swamped at the library, what with Christmas coming up. We had a class in today, from Edison School, working on their planets book reports and the Mama Goose Story Time at ten. Judy is on vacation and, Lori is acting head librarian. She takes the role a little too seriously, if you ask me. I mean, she's actually arguing with me about book choice. I planned to read *The Snowman* and she told me it's too advanced of a book for the one-to-three-year-olds. I tried to explain to her how I could improvise, but she worked up a real sweat over it.

"Fine," I said. "What do you suggest?"

"How about *Santa's Busy Night*?"

"There's a classic," I mumbled, but I took it.

When we're too busy for me to take lunch at the usual time I almost self-destruct in front of the poor mother who just wants a copy of the *Polar Express*. I'm so not present for work. I'm making all these stupid mistakes and saying "huh" so many times that finally Lori said, "What's with you today? Are you sick or something?"

"Yeah," I lied, "I woke up with a sore throat." I was thinking this is how I'll get out of here. But you know old Lori. You really want to be bleeding all over her actual shoes if you want to be sent home.

"I've got a cough drop in my purse," she said.

"Thanks," I said. "That'll be great."

Really, I mean, you don't even want some terminal illness diagnosis 'cause she'll just be like, "How long do they say you have?" so she can estimate just how many books you'll be able to shelve before you keel over. Finally, around quarter of two, as I'm about to chew my ow arm off, I got a lunch break.

I'm supposed to meet Henry after work. We're meeting over at the fire station to pick out a Christmas tree, and Betsy's at home making this great stew she makes every year with lots and lots of red wine in it. If we're lucky she'll make bread. The stew is a staple of the tree-raising night. The bread is an elective, depending on what kind of day she's had with the kindergarteners, all high on candy canes and Christmas "gimmes." It was one of those things, the stew, after Betsy came back, that made me feel like my life was finally starting a new chapter, that maybe we'd all make it after all, that we wouldn't just be these three pathetic people—Henry and I walking around all dazed and shuffling, and Kate flying in and out of rooms like some trapped bird.

The fire station was a mad house. The guys strung Christmas lights all haphazardly along the building and in the parking lot. It was dark and kids were chasing each other, screaming, in and out of the rows of trees, and the whole place smelled of pine. It practically knocks you over, the smell's so rich and swirling. Henry likes the medium-sized trees—nothing too grandiose, nothing too "Charlie Brownish"—so I headed in that direction. On my way over there I saw Randy carrying some tree to a woman's car, a length of thick twine in his hand, dragging along on the ground behind him.

"Hey, Randy," I called to him.

He looked around to see who it was and, when he spotted me, yelled back, "Hey, May. Hang out. I'll be right back."

I smiled, nodding, and kept walking toward the medium trees.

Then an electric saw started going and when I looked over toward the noise I saw first the glimmer of metal, and then I was thinking, *God, look at that guy. He's cutting that tree with one arm and that other metal arm.* Then he finished the fresh cut and hoisted the tree over his shoulder. It was when he started walking away, the gait itself, that I realized it was Buddy.

"Hey, May."

I jumped and Randy was standing next to me. He draped his arm over my shoulder, gave me a squeeze.

"So, you found him," he said after a second.

I nodded slowly, not taking my eyes off Buddy as he headed toward a yellow Honda and started helping the guy tie the tree to the hood. "When did he get back in town?"

"About a week and a half ago. We keep givin' him shit, telling him he needs to call you, start groveling immediately so maybe you'll take him back sometime before he retires."

"But what's he doing? I mean—"

"You mean with his arm?"

"Yeah." I could see him pulling the rope tight, making these knots, using the arm like he'd had it his whole life. As amazed as I was to see Buddy, I just couldn't keep my eye off the arm, the way it moved, and the metallic flashes in the light.

"Dispatcher. Kevin called him down in Mexico and told him to get his ass back up here, that we all had heard what a loser he was with a rod. And you know Buddy and Kevin, they go back, and really Kevin wasn't asking. I'd heard from Hawke, that he wasn't making it, that it was just him being stubborn and angry that was keeping him down there. I was there when Kevin called him. He told him, 'I'll come down there and pick your sorry ass up if I have to,' and you could just practically hear

Buddy on the other end going, 'Yes, sir. Okay, sir,' all hound-doggish. Two days later he was here. Has he seen you?"

"No," I said softly, like he might hear me over all the noise, and for a second I thought to run. That I needed to get away, go run behind the station and lean against the cold cement wall, catching my breath.

Randy was still talking. "Yeah, well, wait till he sees you."

And as if Buddy had heard him, he turned from the car with one last tug on the rope.

"Hey, Cane!" Randy yelled to him, pointing his thumb at me.

Buddy looked blank for a second, like he was trying to place me, but then he smiled, one of those slow, quizzical Buddy smiles that can look like a hug, and started toward us.

"Be easy on him, May," Randy said. "Remember, the guy's crazy for you."

"Oh, yeah? I guess he has his own secret way of showing it." Even as the words were coming out of my mouth I could hear Betsy saying, "Don't be so stubborn, May. It's an emotion that leaves you lonely and stuck," like she was reasoning with one of her third-graders.

Buddy was wearing the blue Alameda Fireman T-shirt with the little white helmet on the chest and the station number under it, and then he had one of those Santa Claus pins that lights up. I pulled the string, smiling as it glowed.

"There she goes, yanking your chain," Randy said.

"Jesus Christ, Brouwer, can't you get lost or something?" Buddy gave him a shove, but we laughed anyway, because Randy's always such a goof, because we were nervous and because of the grain of truth. "How you doing, May?" Buddy said, and I finally looked up at him.

"Good. I mean, there's stuff going on with Kate—"

"There's always stuff going on with Kate."

"Yeah." I rolled my eyes. "But yeah, other than that everything is good, great."

"I heard you got your Master's, got a job at the library."

"Yeah, I'm one of the children's librarians at the main branch."

"That's great. You still see Cathy?"

"Oh, yeah. I mean, sure, when she's in town."

And we were both glancing around, trying to find something else to say, obviously so stupidly nervous, I was feeling like one real moron.

"That Cathy," Randy chimed in, "she's cute. I mean in a tomboyish kind of way. She have a boyfriend?"

"They just broke up."

"Great. I mean, that's too bad."

"Excuse me, I hate to interrupt but I think I have you two clowns on the payroll." I turned around to see Kevin. "Hi, dear," he said, giving me a kiss on the cheek and a pat on the arm. "Are these men bothering you, miss?"

"Hi, Kevin. How are you?"

"Great. Selling those trees for the kids and we got a room full of gifts people've been bringing. How's your family?"

"Fine." I figured I didn't really want to get into the Kate thing with Kevin and Randy standing around anyway.

"So, you see what the cat dragged in?" He pointed to Buddy. "As stubborn as the day is long, but we're gonna make his sorry butt into a dispatcher yet. None of my business, May, but you gotta let the guy take you out and then, as soon as you can, find a friend for this other sorry sack. The two of them are driving me crazy. I'm telling you, it's a pitiful sight, them hanging around the station on their day off, washing their cars, 'Hey, Sarge, you wanna play rummy?' You hear what I'm saying? It's pathetic."

"I'll see what I can do." I smiled.

"You're a good girl, May. Now you," he said, turning on Randy, "you may not have noticed but we're open for another half-hour." He called to a man and a little boy behind Randy, "Yes, sir. This man will get you all set up." Then he whispered in my ear, "Remember, go easy on him."

"May, I see your Dad over there. I'll go over and help him pick out something nice, tell him where you are," Kevin said.

"Thanks, Kevin. Tell him I'll be right there." And when he walked away I let out a big breath. "Wow," I said, "that was a little intense."

"God." Buddy ran his hand through his hair. I made a special effort not to look at the metal arm. And we just stood there looking at each other. "It's good to see you, May."

"It's good to see you, too."

And then we stood there some more, but before one of us started shuffling feet Buddy said, "You want to maybe go grab some breakfast tomorrow morning, catch up a little?"

"Sure—oh, God, no. You know what? I can't. I have plans."

"With your boyfriend?"

"How'd you know I have a boyfriend?"

"Randy. He saw you guys over at Noah's having lunch. I mean, Kevin's right, we haven't been real busy."

I shook my head. "Okay, yeah, with my boyfriend. Well, I don't know if he's my boyfriend. We're kind of old for that. He's this guy I'm seeing. Scott. That's his name." Why was I getting all fumbly? I wasn't the one who disappeared for three years. I was allowed to have a boyfriend or someone I see or whatever you call it. "Anyway, I'm busy, but I'd love to go to breakfast. Could we go Sunday?"

"Sure. It's good to see you, May. You look great."

"So do you."

"Except for the arm, right?"

"It's no big deal, Buddy."

"Oh, yeah? Then why won't you look at it. Hey, whatever, ignore me. I'm just nervous. It's just good to see you. I've said that already, huh?"

"A couple times, yeah." And then I cracked up because Randy was making the big loser sign with his hand over his forehead while a woman counted bills into his other outstretched hand.

Buddy mouthed "fuck you" to him and then turned to me. "Jim's?"

"Yeah."

"Around ten?"

"Sure."

"Okay, I'll see you Sunday morning."

And when we hugged good-bye, Buddy felt just the same to me and smelled of pine.

I followed Henry back to the house, reaching into my bag a couple times to feel the cover of the journal, rubbing the rough fabric. Why would he keep this from us? Or had he not known about it? After all, the box was labeled "taxes." As I pulled into the driveway behind him I decided I wasn't going to say anything tonight, that I wanted to know more, read more, before I talked to him about it.

"I smell bread," he said, slamming the car door and untying the cord that secured the tree to the hood. I sniffed the cakey smell of Betsy's bread and the deep wine aroma of the stew and suddenly I was starving.

Henry and I lifted the tree off the hood and carried it through the garage.

"Dinner in five," Betsy called from the kitchen, "and, May, Scott called, wants you to call him tonight if you can. His number's by the phone."

I thought, *Oh, God, yeah, Scott.* I felt like I was floating between three worlds tonight—my mother's, my old life with Buddy and the present. The smell of the pine and bread and stew were like a rich steamy cloud around me. I sighed deeply, even shook my head to clear it, and that helped a bit.

"Did you find a nice tree?" Betsy asked, coming into the dining room and placing a bowl of salad on the table. "Oh, that's a nice one." She peered into the living room at the tree. "Much nicer than that poor little orphan you brought home last year, dear." She gave Henry a quick peck.

"That was a perfectly good tree."

Betsy just raised an eyebrow at me as she headed back to the kitchen.

I smiled. "And guess who we saw at the station? Buddy."

"Oh, really." Her head popped out of the kitchen. "Did you talk to him?"

"We're having breakfast on Sunday." I came into the kitchen and took the breadbasket from her.

"That's nice. I always liked Buddy." She handed Henry the tureen, steaming, the glass top cloudy. "Okay, let's eat."

I felt the usual gratitude for Betsy's tact, the way she knows to give you your space, let you figure your own world out. When I was a teenager I'd sometimes try to get her to tell me what to do—so I could have the arguments I'd hear about from my friends—but Betsy wouldn't ever bite.

It was when we sat down, when we were passing the salad bowl and breadbasket, ladling stew, that I thought to miss Kate, that I even remembered she was gone. A little shot of fear went through me. In the same way I used to worry I would forget my mother if I lost the T-shirt in my underwear drawer. And I thought, it'd be Christmas soon, and we'd be opening presents and there'd be no Kate, and no Kate always looking prettier than me in the more perfect black New Year's dress. And as always, I wondered what in the world she could be thinking, to miss all this, to make herself lost like this when the two of us knew too well what lost really feels like—a little girl making her way through the world without a mother. Betsy and Henry were talking about whether to put lights up this year, and I drank in their voices, ate some of the hot stew, dunked the warm buttery bread. My chest hurt, squeezed tight with missing Kate.

I found myself wanting to leave. I cleared the table, put coffee on while Betsy placed tins of Christmas cookies on the coffee table, yet we were only halfway through the decorating when I just had to go.

"I just can't get sick right now." I pursed my lips in fake nausea. "It's so busy at work and I haven't done a third of my Christmas shopping." Within minutes I was out the door with a baggy of shortbread cookies and a warm Tupperware container of stew.

It was when I was leaning back in the tub, my back pressing against the cool porcelain, that I felt it. I reached back into the warm water and touched the spot high on my back, rubbed it with two fingers, thinking, *That's got to be a bruise for sure*. And in those same seconds I remembered Kate's closet and the hook, and I remembered Kate's bruise. *Of course that's how she got her bruise.* I closed my eyes, breathed in the warm lavender steam. *Oh, Kate.*

I put on the thickest flannel pajamas I have and crawled into bed with the journal.

Chapter 13

4-23-72

Mother and Father arrived tonight with my suitcases packed. I leave tomorrow morning. They were dressed to go to a dinner party at the Hennleys' and Mother kept reaching up to touch her pearls where they lay in two strands at the base of her throat, as if they might have fallen off from one moment to the next. Every now and then she would nod absently as Father went over again what was happening.

"So, Liza, your mother and I—in consultation with Dr. Lane, I might add—have decided you will go to Pennsylvania. There is a residence there, a reputable one, run by the Sisters the Good Shepherd. You will stay there until the baby is born and then you will go ahead and begin Bryn Mawr for the second semester. I've spoken with the dean and explained that you were given the opportunity to take a trip through Europe with your mother and I, and they've agreed to let you postpone your admission by one semester."

It was if someone had slapped me out of a deep sleep because my first thought was, oh, yes, a baby. *I hadn't forgotten I was pregnant; I just hadn't followed that, I suppose, to its logical conclusion of an actual baby.*

"We think this is the best solution and I'm asking you to obey me on this without giving me any more trouble because, quite frankly, Liza, I'm at my wit's end with you."

"Okay, Father," I said, because I don't suppose I really cared. He looked surprised and pleased.

"There's a good girl," he said, petting my hair. "You'll put all this behind you, and a year from now you'll be having a grand time at college."

And when they left Mother kissed me on the cheek and said, "I packed your favorite dress and your blue jeans, and I had Vicky put a tin of her oatmeal cookies in the smaller suitcase to share with the other girls." She wasn't even looking at me and before she turned to leave she patted my arm like she was drumming her fingers on a countertop. If I know Mother she was thinking about what she would say to the Hennleys and the Parkers at dinner tonight, what she could possibly tell them about her impossible trial of a daughter.

4-24-72

I feel like I've come here to die. This place is as silent and shiny as a coffin. I counted twelve girls at dinner, although I'm to have a roommate who Sister Nancy told me would not arrive until next weekend. This place flutters and shimmers in front of my eyes like heat rising off the hot street. I know some of this is just exhaustion from the flight and nausea and disbelief that in a day I am in another state, but I think more truly in another world. The whole place even smells like nothing I've ever known. My room is a sparse rectangle with two iron beds and two plain wooden dressers. It's too dark to see any view from the window.

4-25-72

The smell is Murphy's Oil Soap. I would know as I spent the morning rubbing circles on stair after stair and then almost broke my own neck from the slickness. These poor girls. I'm not far enough along yet to look pregnant but most of the others are. Their bodies look like so many ripe melons. In comparison to the sparseness of this place they are almost a shock, lush and sinful. I know they feel like this because they all walk around with their eyes glued to the floor or steal a quick glance and dart their eyes away again. One girl—I don't know a single name yet since we ate breakfast and lunch in complete silence—can't be more than 13, a bird of a thing with drab stringy hair the color of pale skin.

There is one small sitting room with two worn red plaid tweed couches and a coffee table. I read this month's Time *magazine and yesterday's* Philadelphia Inquirer. *It was so good to see something about the rest of the world. There was a small TV in the corner and when I flipped it on the news was on. I sat watching it and then, suddenly, I saw Sister Christine in the doorway. I nearly jumped out of my skin, as I was sure television was somehow forbidden, but she actually sat down with me and watched it. The anchorman mentioned something about the Olympics.*

"I love the gymnastics," she said, smiling. "I used to love to do cartwheels." She must have seen the surprise on my face because she added, "I was a terrible tomboy as a young girl." I so like Sister Christine. I'm so glad she's my Sister.

4-26-72

I seem to have a gift for polishing wood, God help me. I was cleaning the paneling leading up the stairwell, these furious little circles 'round and 'round, and Sister Nancy came up the stairs, paused and said to me, this serene hint of a smile, "Lovely work, Liza."

I just rolled my eyes at her and smiled back. I wonder if you go to hell for getting fresh with a nun? No matter. She smiled right back like she understood how absurd the whole thing is. Besides, I'm not going to be like those other girls who won't look the nuns in the eye. I have nothing to be ashamed of. At least I'm attractive enough to get pregnant—not like these nuns who look like bald men. Oh, God, do you go to hell for insulting nuns? That's the problem with living with nuns, you think of hell all the time.

I was done by 4 p.m. and set off for a walk through the grounds. We're fenced in here like sheep, high black iron fence and a huge swinging gate in the front. It must be acres of woods toward the back. I've never seen such greenness, the tiniest pale green buds on the tips of tree branches and flower beds filled with the little fronds of some kind of plant or flower poking out from the dirt. In the right side yard is a long covered walkway, a trellis on top with bare tangled branches weaving in and out. The lawn itself is speckled green and brown and there's a small cemetery, maybe a hundred tombstones, along the back corner of the grounds. The air smells different here, damp, mossy, and it's the strangest feeling to be at once chilled by an icy wind and warmed by the sun.

I sat on a bench, my eyes closed, my face held up to the sun like an offering. I was tired from, oh, I think everything. I must have dozed off because I thought it was a minute or two but I opened my eyes to barely catch the sky going from pink to gray and hurried back inside to wash for dinner. I am tired so deeply these days it's as if my blood, and even my hair, are even tired and yet it's a nice tired, a downy lap kind of tired.

4-27-72

More wood to polish. I'm a little less interested in being the Polishing Whore of the Year as I'm beginning to get a cramp in my right shoulder. Luckily, I started classes today. Seems that every morning from 8 a.m. until noon there are classes. Today we had English Literature and are reading Shakespeare. We read Shakespeare at Marlborough and I didn't like it any better then. I think if you have something to say you should just come out and say it and not take refuge behind a bunch of confusing sentences and words just to prove you're smart. That's how I feel about it anyway. But Sister Mary Katherine obviously would disagree. She practically got up on her desk during one part of Hamlet. *We're supposed to read the rest tonight but I'm not. I know what happens. He dies. I think a lot of other people die too and if I could understand what they were saying I might actually care. After that class we do grammar for an hour and at the end of that I was so fidgety and bored I hid in the bathroom. Thankfully we can go to the bathroom anytime we want—being pregnant and all. When I came back they were singing, but there was someone new I hadn't seen before, a Sister Helen, the only Sister I've seen so far who doesn't appear to be seventy years old. I think she may be a new nun because she can't be more than twenty. She must have just gotten here. I would have noticed her since she is the only one here who is not pregnant or wrinkled.*

It appears that there is some structure here that I'm not quite privy to but I gather Sister Christine is my assigned nun. I think she is one of the oldest—maybe even a hundred so. I'm not getting too attached to her as she could die on me at any time. Our paths manage to cross every day and today she asked me if I'd like to rake leaves with Sister Helen. Of course. Anything to be outside, away from Shakespeare and wood polish. I'm to meet Sister Helen by the front door of the convent directly after lunch tomorow. Sister Christine told me Sister Helen is an accomplished gardener and I could learn much from her. Sister Christine would know—she probably tended the Garden of Eden.

4-28-72

Sister Helen is twenty-one. I was sitting on the bottom step by the front door (my lower back is starting to ache) and she just seemed to appear, standing in front of me.

"Hello, Liza. I'm Sister Helen," she said so formally I leaped up and shook her hand, which clearly startled her, and I felt like such a social idiot.

There's a rather large shed behind the convent that I hadn't noticed before. It smells of damp dirt, cut grass and gasoline. Someone's job must be to clean its windows because small as they are, they light up the shed. She handed me a rake and a tarp and took two rakes for herself. As we walked out to the first flower bed she asked, "Have you raked before?"

I got quite insulted before I realized that, in fact, I hadn't raked before. "No, I guess not."

"Oh, that's okay," she said, smiling. "I'll show you."

And it's really not terribly hard at all.

She has a sweet moon of a face, with pale eyes the color of grocery bags. It's hard to tell with her hair covered by her habit but she may be quite pretty.

"Henry Simpson will be here any minute so between the three of us I expect we'll get most of this side yard done by suppertime."

Well, you can imagine how my mouth dropped open. I didn't know they allowed an actual non-priest, non-marble-statue male on the grounds. By the time this Henry arrived she had maneuvered me to the far end of the yard with my rake and tarp. Henry started on the opposite end, which I'm sure was no coincidence. Really! As if we'd fall together like dogs right there on the lawn. As if he'd even be interested in pregnant me. You have to wonder if someone like Sister Helen ever has feelings for men. Of what I could see of Henry Simpson he wasn't bad looking at all, a little taller and skinnier than the boys I like to date, but not homely at all, with thick brown hair.

I picked a bunch of the new tulips that sprung up this week and brought them to Marcy. I was going to ask her to put them in a vase for my room but she looked so pleased I handed the vase back to her and said, "They're for you," even though I hadn't intended that. She just beamed at me and threw her arms around me. Honestly, I almost started to cry. It's been so long since anyone has touched me. And then—maybe it was the hug or the tulips but I remembered. "It's my birthday tomorrow."

Marcy pulled away, her hands on my shoulders. She suddenly looked so sad.

"I'm eighteen," I told her. "I'm a grown-up."

4-29-72

I didn't say a word to anyone about my birthday but at supper Marcy brought out a birthday cake. Joanne jumped up and turned off the lights and they all sang to me—and I sat there, hating it, trying not to cry. When I got up to my room there was a card on my bed. I recognized Mother's handwriting. "Happy Birthday to a Darling Daughter. Love, Mother and Father." And fifty dollars. I stood over my little trash can and let first the envelope and then the card fall in, one at a time, each making a soft tap as it hit the bottom of the can.

Still, when I came back from washing up there was another envelope slid under my door. It had a picture of an angel shimmering and smiling down on a girl and when I opened the card it said simply, "Happy Birthday. May the Lord bless and guide you on your journey." All the Sisters had signed it. I propped it up on my nightstand and went to bed.

5-1-72

I met Father Michael yesterday. He is the priest. He hears confession for all the girls on Saturday, holds Mass at the church on Sunday morning and then attends Sunday dinner. I couldn't eat a bite, I was so nervous and—for the first time—almost ashamed. I think I will just pretend to be sick next weekend to avoid the whole ordeal. Honestly, it feels like they have him for dinner just to ensure we feel shameful and bad.

Helen is from Massachusetts, a little town near Boston. That's why she has the strange, thick accent. Her favorite color used to be blue but now she doesn't have a favorite color or food since she's given everything up to God. Marcy, the cook, packs us a lunch now that the weather is so nice, and Henry meets us and we all sit under the huge walnut tree to eat. That's when we talk. At first I thought Helen was purposefully trying to keep her distance from us, but really she is just shy. And Henry is quiet but sweet. It's always me that starts the games. What's your favorite color? What's your favorite movie? If you had three wishes what would they be? Of course, Helen has three wishes about God. Finally today I just said, "Yes, yes, we know, God is all things, but what about after God?"

"Oh, there is nothing after God."

Henry just looked down at his sandwich and smiled but I couldn't help myself.

"I know you don't believe that for a minute. And you can't possibly feel it. You can't just be God's servent, Helen. You have to be Helen and then you can serve God."

I have no idea where that came from but it hurt her feelings, I could tell. So, I just said, "You're going to be a great nun, Helen."

And Henry nodded. I wish Henry would speak up sometimes.

Henry's family owns a farm about a mile from the convent. Henry walks here. If I can find a way, one day I want to go see it. I'm not a prisoner but it just seems like all the other girls don't leave. I'm not ashamed and I need to get out. I need to do some shopping. So, I'm going to ask Sister Christine if I can walk home with Henry tomorrow. I mean, honestly, I'm pregnant, what more could go wrong? I was saying today to them that my stomach is really pooching out now and Henry asked, "Where's the father?"

So, I told them both about James and how we're going to be married as soon as he is able to get here. I got a letter from Rachel and she told me James calls her all the time asking about me and that a letter is coming from him soon. It will say where we can meet and how we will marry. I've written four letters but I never hear back. I know his mother is getting the letters before he gets home from school but Rachel tells him I am writing so he knows.

"Do you have a girlfriend?" I asked Henry.

"Maureen," he said, "but she died."

"Died?"

"Leukemia," he said, and I could tell that was all he wanted to say. He's leaving for California in the fall to go to college at Berkeley, and he's never been out of this town.

I laughed when he told me. "Oh, Henry, you'll never come back here."

And then we raked and weeded all afternoon until the sky started to turn colors and the air got cooler. We should be done by tomorrow and then we won't be out again until it's time to plant the flowers. Helen said we're going to start growing little seeds.

5-6-72

When I asked Sister Christine about going to the farm she paused and I knew she was going to say no. I should have been quiet but I couldn't help it. I just said, "Please! You have to let me! I promise to be good," and I couldn't help it, but my eyes started to tear up.

She pursed her lips, thinking, and then she said carefully, "If Sister Helen is willing to accompany you, yes, you may go."

I wanted to hug her. I could tell Sister Helen and Henry were surprised when I told them.

"What did you say to her?" Sister Helen asked, her eyes wide with amazement.

"Nothing. I just asked if I could go. I told her how much I wanted to see the farm. Oh, you must come along, Sister Helen. Or else I can't go. You're the chaperone, Sister Helen, so Henry and I don't get into any trouble." This made them both blush. Honestly. Sometimes I feel like I'm with two old ladies.

The farm is for cows and goats and sheep. There are baby animals of all kinds coming, and even some chicks that were born recently. They run around the coop like little puffs of yellow and when you catch one they peep frantically and tremble. In the coop, out of nowhere, Henry said, "How did you get pregnant anyway?" I don't know how I must of looked at him because I couldn't believe what he said, but he sighed and shrugged. "I mean, I know how it happens, but didn't you think you'd get pregnant? Weren't you afraid?"

"No," I told him, "I was too in love to think about that."

"That's not very smart, Liza."

This made me mad. "Oh, don't be so smug, Henry, just because you were too afraid to do it with Maureen." When I realized what I said my hand flew over my mouth, but it was too late. He swung around to say something to me, then didn't. He walked out of the coop with me calling, "Oh, Henry, I'm so sorry." But he just kept walking. I say the meanest, stupidest things sometimes.

Sister Helen would only say, "Tomorrow after church you can apologize again, Liza, after he's had a night to forgive. Henry's a good, Catholic boy. He knows about forgiveness."

But I think maybe I don't deserve to be forgiven.

5-17-72

Mother sent a box of maternity clothes. When I called to thank her she just said, "I thought you must have grown out of the others by now." She's right, I have. Just my breasts and my stomach so you can't really tell but I could hardly get my dresses zipped and my jeans buttoned.

And then I don't know why I said it but I said, "I miss you and Daddy."

"Well, Liza, I'm afraid that's the price you pay for your actions." Her words made me start to cry. I know she doesn't miss me, that I disappoint her and she's probably relieved to have me away. That's fine. I'm not going back there anyway.

Sister Helen asks me every day if I want to go to the farm to apologize to Henry and I just can't. I tell her this and she looks at me all stern and says, "I suppose you'll want to be praying on this some more then." I rolled my eyes and went back to raking but I glanced over, toward the road, where I could see Henry, up on a ladder, on the other side of the hedge, snippets of hedge flying in the air and the clicking of the trimmer. He keeps away from me as much as he can. He won't even look at me.

9:00 p.m.

I can't sleep. I keep thinking about James and what Mother said. And then I started thinking about this baby. I wonder what will happen to her. I think it's a her. I wonder what her parents will be like, if she'll get into trouble like me. I wonder if I will miss her, if I'll even get to see her. And then I wonder what it would be like to be a mother—not like my mother but maybe like Rachel's mother, who smiles at Rachel with her whole face and pats her hair. Maybe one day when I'm older I will be a mother but for now I just want to, need to, be back with James.

Chapter 14

"The problem with fishing is that there's too much quiet and waiting and sitting. And it wasn't exactly like we were cleaning up or anything." Buddy closed his menu. "What are you having?"

"Waffle Special."

"Still?"

I shrugged.

"Yeah, me too," he said. "So anyway, then Kevin calls . . ." He drifted off and for a second we both just sipped our coffee. "Well, shit, you know the rest."

"About being a dispatcher? Do you like it?"

And he smirked at me like I knew better than that. And I did.

"Is it too hard to be there, you mean?" I asked.

"You know, May, anything's better than sitting on a boat waiting for some fish to take pity on you and eat your bait. I mean, having your future hanging on something that's going to be a filet someday can just get demeaning. Really. You start to think these kinds of things when you're sitting around all day. The dispatcher thing, that's different. Being back with the guys, the sounds, Randy's lousy pork chops, all that's—I can't even tell you—that's the best. It's when we get a call and everyone's running and the sound of the trucks starting up and it's just go, go, go and every time I think—inside you know—I'm going. But I'm not. Then they pull out—and I'm still sitting there—just like on the boat."

"Oh, Buddy."

"That's the thing I can't get past. I try. I really do. To not be angry, to feel lucky I'm even alive, and I think I'm okay and then the siren and—I'm sorry, May. I didn't mean to go on like that, lay all this on you the first time we see each other again."

"You know what, Buddy? You think I don't know this? You think anyone who loved you the way I did doesn't know exactly how this would feel for you. Before you left all I was asking was for you to say these things to me, to let me in, and you just wouldn't. And I kept trying and I got angrier and angrier and you got further and further away—and then you were gone."

And, of course, that was when the waitress decided to show up with the friggin' waffles, and I wouldn't look up at her when she asked about more coffee because the tears were sitting like big blurry ponds on my eyes.

"I'm sorry, May," he said when she finally left.

"You should be." I wiped my eyes with my fingertips. "And I *promised* myself I wasn't going to do this."

"No. I was a jerk. You be as angry as you want."

"Don't worry. I have been angry—about you leaving, about the time that's gone by, even angry about how you messed up my plans to get married right after college. But it hasn't really gotten me anywhere." I paused then, pushing my waffle around with my fork, thinking. "When you left, your mom said something to me that I always think about, about how you have to make peace with this if you're going to be any good for anyone, including yourself. I guess that's it. I worry that all this will eat away at you, if you let it, and ten, twenty years from now you'll be someone I won't even know."

He just nodded and neither one of us seemed to know what to say. It felt all heavy and sad then, but true just the same.

"I know that I still love you, May. The other stuff I'm figuring out."

"Sure. Of course you are. I don't even know what I'm saying. You know, with my mom and all, I'm the last one to sit here and give directions on how to figure anything out. If you only knew—"

"What?"

And so I told him about Kate, even my mother's journal. "And we don't even know anyone in Long Island."

"I guess Kate does."

"I guess."

When the waitress brought the check I reached for it. Buddy beat me to it. "Oh, come on, May. Give me a break. I heard what you said. I promise I won't consider it a date if you let me pay. I mean, I know about Scotty and all."

"Scott," I corrected him. "Scotty is a little dog."

"Yeah, yeah, sorry. Scott. So does he know we're having breakfast?"

"I don't think he needs to know that."

"If it was me I'd be needing to know that."

"That's different, Buddy."

"Like how?"

"Like Scott and I are just dating. We're not engaged or anything." I didn't know why I kept getting all flustered. I had every right to be dating and then it occured to me. "Are you seeing anyone?"

"Why do you ask?" he said, all like he was giving me a hard time.

"As in, you know my situation. I thought it would only be sporting of you to tell me yours," I said as he held the door open and we walked onto the street.

"'Sporting'? Is that a word you picked up from Scott?"

"You know what, Buddy? In the time you've been gone I could have picked up a new language."

"Fair enough," he said as I gave him a little shove. "But really," he said all quiet, looking right at me, when we got to my car, "I would like to take you out. Like a real date. Somewhere nice for dinner. Why don't you think about it? I know what I'm asking, May, for you to give me another chance."

I covered my face with my hands, shaking my head, kind of groaning, kind of laughing, because those were the words I'd been waiting to hear for years, played them over and over in my head, and now that I heard them it was so clear they weren't enough. They didn't even begin to untangle everything that had happened and I couldn't even believe how stupid and naïve I could be sometimes. Just then I felt Buddy's arm around me, pulling me toward him, and I rested my head on his chest. We stood there like that with all the Park Street traffic going by.

"We can have dinner," I said, "but it's just dinner, Buddy. I don't know about any chances. I don't know about any of that."

I pulled away slowly, squinting into the sunlight. I could tell by the look on his face that he didn't like that but he just said, "Okay. And I'm not."

"Not what?"

"Seeing anyone."

He stood there on the sidewalk as I drove away, and I kept looking back at him through my rearview mirror. All these sad, hard feelings stuck in my throat, the kind where if you talk you cry. I never stopped loving Buddy, even when I hated him, even when I would have days at a time when I wouldn't think about him. It just stopped hurting so much.

"You're not going to get that off. Just forget it. I'm telling you, it's not coming off." Jamie handed me a wet dishtowel. I scrubbed away at my pant leg anyway.

"This is why," Rich said from the couch, where he was cradling little Charles in his arms, "you keep seeing us in these ratty old things. I'm not ruining one more shirt. The baby barf does not come out."

And as if to chime in with his father, Charles let out what I'm sure to him was a scream but sounded more like a hungry kitten.

"Okay, okay, Charlie, let's go change the diapy and see about putting you down," Rich said, standing up with him. He held Charles out so we could all plant a kiss on top of his tiny little head and smell his sweet powdery skin and formula-breath smell.

Sighing, Jamie flopped down on the couch next to me and picked his glass of wine up off the coffee table.

"Tired?" Cathy asked

"Girl, if I was any more tired I'd just be in a coma. We'll be home by nine for sure—if we make it that long."

"Oh, try to stay out," Cathy urged. "We want time for him to wake up so we can give him a bottle."

"Why don't you just stay and you can give him his three a.m. bottle?"

I ruffled Jamie's hair and he leaned into me, sliding down, his head in my lap.

"It's unbelievable though," he said, his eyes closed, "even at three in the morning. You can't even believe how amazing. Unbelievable . . . even though it leaves you with no vocabulary."

"It sounds wonderful," I said, and I meant it. I want kids so bad sometimes, thought I'd at least have a couple by now back when Buddy and I were engaged.

"So anyway," he said, sitting up, "give me the quickie on Buddy before I go in and get ready. He's back?"

"And more so, wanting our girl back," Cathy added.

"Wait," Rich called from the hall, "I have to hear this. He's out like a light," he told Jamie, as he snuggled onto the couch next to him. "Okay, I'm ready. So?"

And they were all looking at me. I sighed. "It's not that good of a story."

"May! Let me tell it," Cathy said, "Okay, so she goes to meet Henry to get the Christmas tree at the fire station and guess who's there . . ."

As she replayed the story I remembered it like a movie—how close he stood, the way his hair was all messed up, the smell of coffee all the guys have at the station and then his words at Jim's—*I know what I'm asking, May, for you to give me another chance.*

And I didn't know. I just didn't know. She must have finished telling the story because they were all looking at me.

"So, are you seeing him again?" Jamie asked.

"Yes. I mean, I think so. He said he wanted to take me to dinner. So,

I guess if he actually calls me we'll go out to dinner."

The three of them were nodding, all serious, like this was a wise and prudent plan.

"Can I ask you something?" Rich asked. "And you can just come over here and slap me if you want, but does it bother you, him only having one arm? I mean, it must be strange."

"It's the weirdest thing. It's like part of me doesn't even notice because it's just Buddy. It felt this way when he first lost his arm. I don't know what to do, like how to hug him or reach for him or even sometimes where to look, and so I worry I'm making him uncomfortable. The whole time in the restaurant you could hardly tell one of his arms was missing because he was eating with the other hand but then when he went to pay the bill, he took his wallet out of his pocket. He just used the—jeez, I don't even know what you call it—the prosthesis—like it's just his other hand. But I don't know . . ." I stared into the dark hallway. "I guess I don't know what I feel about it . . . or Buddy."

And I must have looked pretty damn pathetic 'cause they all gave me these sad half-smiles.

Jamie squeezed my shoulder. "We love you, honey. We know how hurt you were. Just take it slow."

"And keep us posted," Rich put in. "We can spot you. Save you from yourself and your poor judgment in men."

Jamie kicked him.

"All right," Jamie said, "I'm going to get ready."

I got to feed Charlie his bottle in the dark quiet of his room, with just this dim little nightlight on the other side of the room so I could barely see his eyes, closed and slightly fluttering, and the sweet little sucking sounds. I rocked us back and forth in the glider and all of it made me feel sort of floaty and sleepy in the most wonderful way. The bottle was pretty big, given how little he was, but he was working away at it like he might slam it down on the armrest when he was done and call, "Another over here, Sal."

I have this other memory of my mother from when I was about three and I had this really high fever. Even I knew I was way sick, and she lifted me, all sweaty and squinting, from the bed to the bathroom. It must have been pretty late because the whole house was dark. She closed the door and set me down on the tile floor and I held onto her leg because I felt like I might fall.

"Let's pretend, May, that you are a lovely hot bowl of chocolate pudding, too hot to eat, that we need to cool off."

"I want chocolate pudding."

"Okay, but let's pretend *you're* the pudding and we're going to put you in the cool bath so you won't be so hot and we can eat you up."

And I liked that, let her pick me up and place me into the cool water. As my bottom hit the water I shivered and inhaled the alcohol smell. She took a washcloth and squeezed the water over my shoulders, and I watched it run down my tummy.

"Here, honey." She placed two baby aspirins on my tongue and I squished them on the roof of my mouth.

"I'm pudding."

She nodded, running a cool hand through my hair.

For a while she just kept squeezing the washcloth over me, and I could practically see myself getting cool, steam rising off the top of me like pudding or soup. After a bit she lifted me back out and toweled me dry. Then we walked down the stairs and into the kitchen and there *was* pudding. I let out a yelp and climbed up into a chair, watching her every move as she took little Pyrex bowls of pudding out of the refrigerator and two spoons from the drawer. She must have just made the pudding before coming to get me, because it wasn't quite cold, warm spots in the middle.

It's one of the few times I remember being alone with her, without Kate or my father there. Perhaps my mother did give me something good, something I keep inside myself that I can touch for support when I'm a mother, because sometimes the thought of being a mother just terrifies me. Sometimes I remember how she loved me and I don't understand. It's too scary. How can you do that? How can you love like that and then leave or try to kill your own children? I think I know that there's a part of me that is capable of that, that if my own mother was, isn't that inside me too, just like the pudding memory? Maybe it comes out all of a sudden—and before you know it, it takes you over. And you've done it. You're driving off a dock, or a bridge or a cliff, and no one ever can figure out why. It was just this silent monster, lying dormant inside you.

When I looked back down at Charlie, he was asleep, milky drool on his chin and the nipple hanging out of his mouth. I got up and gently placed him in the bassinet, covered him with the yellow blanket.

Chapter 15

6/15/72

I called Rachel today and her mother answered the phone. I wish my mother was so nice. But, of course, she isn't. Rachel wasn't home. She was at Peggy's, but her mother will have her call me later when she gets home. It's a beautiful day today and so after classes and my chores—I'm now back to polishing—I asked Helen—Sister Helen in front of the other nuns—if she would go to the farm with me to see Henry. For all these weeks all he will do is nod at me, without even looking me in the eye, and then, as fast as he can, gets as far away from me as possible. I just feel so terrible about what I said. I found Sister Helen kneeling in the back of the church saying her rosary, so I went and kneeled down next to her. I waited and waited and she kept praying and praying. I had enough time to actually count how far she was—bead thirty-seven—and I wasn't waiting another thirteen so, finally I just whispered, "Helen. Sister Helen."

A minute later when she finished the prayer, she looked over at me. "Yes,

Liza."

"Want to go to the farm?"

"I'm praying."

"You pray all the time. God would want you outside enjoying this beautiful day and helping one of his flock to make amends to another of his flock."

She smiled, shook her head, made the sign of the cross and got up.

An hour later we found Henry in the barn fiddling with some ancient-looking green tractor. Helen went back outside to look at the baby lambs so we could have some privacy.

"Henry, please at least look at me."

"What, Liza?" he said, and he did finally look up at me, but just barely.

"That was a terrible thing for me to say and I'm sorry. I don't know anything about Maureen and I shouldn't have said anything like that anyway. It was mean. I was just feeling—I don't know—ashamed, I guess. It's embarrassing to me to be, ah, pregnant."

He just looked at me for a minute without saying anything. At last he said, "You want to come up here and see something?"

"Sure." He grabbed my hand and helped me up onto the tractor. I peered over into the engine where he was working.

"See?"

"It's an engine."

"No, over here, Liza. This belt. It's busted. We need a new one."

"Is that what you wanted to show me?"

"Yeah."

"Let's go see the lambs. Helen's with the lambs."

"Okay."

All of which I guess meant he accepted my apology. Boys are so strange that way. You never know exactly what they're thinking. Of course, I knew James loved me by his actions but he never really said all the things you would imagine someone would say when he was in love. All the boys I dated acted that way. They call and call and keep asking you out but don't know what to say to a girl except "You're beautiful," which is nice, but sometimes a girl likes to hear that she is loved or what her guy is thinking. The problem with guys is that they tell you what they've done, not how they feel, and mostly I don't care, but when you don't have a lot of girlfriends around it can be boring.

So, we walked over to the lambs. Helen was sitting on a bench, holding a lamb and stroking his back. Just then Mrs. Simpson stuck her head out the backdoor of the house and yelled, "Henry! Find your manners and invite the Sister and that young lady into the house for some coffee."

I looked at Helen to make sure we could actually go in the house and she hopped up from the bench, still holding her lamb, and called back, "Thank you, Mrs. Simpson."

The Simpsons' kitchen is huge with a large wooden table covered in an oilcloth. Mrs. Simpson already had the coffee and cake on the table when we came back from washing our hands. Two little girls sat at the other end of the table.

"This is Katie," Mrs. Simpson said, gesturing to the littlest one who was coloring a picture. "And this is Mary Beth." She looked maybe five years older, around eight, and was doing addition problems.

"Do you like math?" I asked Mary Beth and she nodded vigorously. "That's a pretty picture."

"It's a dragon," Katie said.

We all told her how nice it was which made her puff up and color harder. Mrs. Simpson cut huge pieces of devil's food cake. Her coffee was so much better than at the convent. As she was cutting cake Mr. Simpson came in and washed his hands at the sink. Mrs. Simpson circled the huge table, bringing the cream and sugar to Mr. Simpson, wiping chocolate frosting off of Katie's mouth.

Sitting at the table, Mr. Simpson didn't say much except to ask Henry about the tractor. When Henry told him the trouble he said, "After this we'll go into town to get that belt. We can give the Sister and this young lady a ride back to the convent."

"Thank you, sir," I said, sick of waiting for Helen to speak.

Mr. Simpson smiled back at me."Good cake, huh?"

When we got back to the convent Dr. Price was there. Sister Christine told me I needed to be waiting at the front room in a half an hour for my examination. Helen turned bright pink at that. I just rolled my eyes at her and walked up to my room. Honestly. She's not the one having some strange doctor put his cold hands all over her. I'd seen Dr. Price a couple other times when he came to convent to deliver Mary Tempo's and Lisa Jacobs's babies. Lisa's baby was stillborn and they buried him in the tiniest little white casket out in the back cemetery. She stayed one more week after that and then last night her parents came to take her home. You would think that she would have been so happy, but she looked terrible, the blood all drained from her face and her eyes red-rimmed from crying. I don't really understand. She wasn't going to keep him anyway. I said as much last night, after we watched their car pull away, to my roommate, Joanne, who's a year older and already six months' pregnant. She just looked at me like I had two heads. She looked angry for a minute but then suddenly seemed to think better of it and came to sit next to me on my bed.

"We all try not to think about it so it doesn't hurt so much, but you'll see. Once the baby starts moving it becomes something else altogether and you start thinking."

"Start thinking what?"

"That maybe you'll keep it."

"I won't think that."

"Oh, yes, you will," she said, so quiet and confident that I looked at her.

"How do you know so much?"

"Because I had a baby before. Here. And when the day came to give him away it was like my heart was pulled right out too." She looked out the window and I could tell she was remembering.

"What did they do?" I whispered.

"I told them they had to let me hold him and Sister Christine was there and she told me, in the kindest way you have ever heard, Liza, that I shouldn't, but I insisted." Her voice was wispy and faraway and she didn't look at me, just kept staring out the window. "And when they brought him to me he cried and I held him tight and I cried. And we both just sat in the bed crying at first, but then I leaned down and kissed his little head, over and over, so softly, and he stopped crying and fell asleep. About an hour later he was still sleeping and they came and took him, told me the couple that was adopting him was downstairs and I was screaming, 'No. No.' Sister Margaret was holding me and kept telling me over and over that it was the Lord's wishes and I needed to pray, and then Dr. Price walked in. I remember he stood in the doorway,

staring at me, and then he told the Sisters to leave. When the door closed, for some reason I stopped screaming. He opened his bag and filled a needle with something and said, 'This will help you sleep,' and I can't tell you how badly I wanted to sleep, forever, and when I woke up I wanted to be dead."

She stopped, still not looking at me. Even though I could feel her pain and I knew I should take a step away from it, I couldn't. "But, Joanne, you got pregnant again."

"Yeah . . . and this one is mine."

"But where will you—"

"Don't you tell anyone, Liza."

"I won't," and I meant it. I want Joanne to keep this baby.

She told me more, about another doctor in the next town over, Haverford, who knows families who will take in a girl and her baby while she finds work, that she'd heard this from another girl who was here with her last time. I have a hard time imagining any family willing to do that.

"Do you have money?" I asked.

"No."

"Oh." I didn't tell her I don't think it will work, but I promised myself I'd help her in any way I could. I gave her a hug her and felt her start to cry. "Don't worry, Joanne. You'll keep this baby."

I fetched my purse, where I had a twenty-dollar bill my father sent that week, money that I know my mother has no idea he sends, and I handed it to her.

"Put this away somewhere safe."

"I can't—"

"Yes, you can. You have to."

And she nodded, the bill tight in her fist.

When it was my time to see Dr. Price, I went down to the front room, everything Joanne told me the previous evening playing like a movie in my head. I felt queasy, like I'd been spinning around too much.

Dr. Price is my father's age with thick gray hair. Short and slim, he never says a word during the examinations. Afterward, he always says, "You can get dressed. I'll be back in a minute so we can talk," and walks out into the hallway.

On this particular afternoon, it was dark out the window while I was getting dressed and I could see my reflection. I looked down at my stomach that has become rounded and hard. I cupped a hand under it for a moment, imagining Joanne's lost son, and pulled my hand away.

When Dr. Price came back in the room he sat on the chair opposite me. "You're four months' pregnant. Do you know that?"

I shake my head no.

"Well, you are. Pretty soon you'll start to feel the baby move. That's normal, so you shouldn't worry. I'll see you next month. Do you have any questions?"

"No."

He nodded and I walked out without a word.

"Liza?" he called after me as the door was almost closed. When our eyes met he paused a moment before saying, "Drink milk and nap." He smiled then and I smiled back. He seemed tired.

"Okay." I started to leave again and then blurted, "We're all sad about Lisa. Are you?" I guess I was really wondering if all of us were just these nameless pregnant girls to him, all the same, in the same mess, different ones coming and going but to him might as well be the same.

"Yes, Liza. It's always sad when a baby dies."

I suddenly understand why he looked so tired. I don't know why, but it makes me feel better, like if he can feel sad maybe we matter.

6-22-72

Sister Christine just told me my father is coming tomorrow for a visit. I have no idea why. I tried to call home but no one answered. I suppose I couldn't be in any more trouble than I am.

6-23-72

I cannot bear this. I simply cannot. I keep reading the announcement over and over again to see if it will reveal something more, explain why, but of course it does not. James is marrying someone else. Someone by the name of

Jillian Maple. Father was in New York on business so he took the train from New York to Pennsylvania so he could tell me himself.

"But he loves me!*" I cried when he showed me the newspaper.*

"Apparently not. Or not enough. Sit down, Liza, and calm yourself. This is exactly the kind of thing that happens to girls who—"

"Who are sluts! Is that what you meant to say, Daddy? Well, I know he loved me."

"Liza, it doesn't matter now. Can't you see? Maybe he did love you but Mr. and Mrs. Powell will not be having their son marry a girl who would, would—well, you know exactly what I'm referring to. This girl is from out of town, San Francisco. Very good family, from what I hear, and—"

I stopped listening, let the print blur in front of my eyes and watched my tears fall onto the paper, making dark, wet circles.

"Liza, take this," he said, offering me his handkerchief. "Wipe your eyes. I know this is hard. You make life hard, Liza—for yourself, for us. I don't know why, if it's your sickness—"

I took his handkerchief and wiped my eyes. He was pacing, back and forth, across the dark red carpet, talking almost to himself.

"I really just don't understand. You're such a pretty, smart girl." He sighed, stopping to stare out the window. "Well, I guess that is all. My taxi is here."

"You're leaving already?"

"Yes, I have a plane to catch early in the morning from New York." He reached into his pocket and took out his wallet.

I wanted to scream at him to take his stupid money and choke on it. I hate him, hate them both. I know what they're doing. They're leaving me here so it's easier for them. They say it's for me but I know they want to be rid of me. And that's fine. I want to be rid of me too.

"This is a hundred dollars, Liza. Your mother went shopping this week for more maternity clothes for you. It's not easy for her. She had to go to the Neiman's in San Diego so she wouldn't be seen. It was a very long day for her. You should get them in the mail next week."

"Why doesn't she call me?"

"I—"

"Daddy? Why doesn't she love me? Why won't she love me?"

"Your mother loves you, Liza." But he wouldn't look at me.

He picked his coat up off the chair and when he hugged me good-bye I held on too tight, smelling his damp coat, until he pulled away. I watched the door close after him and sank down onto the couch. James was not coming for me. And worse yet, maybe he never planned to come for me. I was so embarrassed and ashamed that when I went upstairs I just handed Joanne the money.

She counted it. "Liza, this is a hundred dollars!"

"You'll need it," I told her, "and more."

"You must need it."

"I don't." I got my coat out of the closet and started putting it on.

"Where are you going? It's after hours."

"I don't care." I walked out of the room and down the stairs.

At the bottom of the stairs, I met Sister Nancy. "It's after hours. Where are you going, Liza?"

I walked right past her, didn't even look at her.

"Liza!"

I slammed the door and I ran into the darkness toward the little light at the front gate. I tripped and fell but I got right back up and kept running, the tears streaming down my face, and when I got to the gate I flung it open and kept running. The moon was almost full and I found the path right away. I wasn't even scared of the noises, the animals rushing around in the leaves. And when I saw the Simpson house, the lights on in the downstairs windows, I sank to the ground, sat there catching my breath, staring into the windows. I wanted to be inside, wanted to be Katie or Mary Beth, little and asleep and good. But I don't think I ever was that good, not even when I was that young. There was always something wrong with me. Always the episodes.

Inside the barn it was so dark I had to feel my way around to where I remembered seeing the tool bench. When I located it I patted the top, searching for the razor I had seen lying toward the back the day I came to apologize to Henry, but I patted and patted and it wasn't there.

"Liza?"

I jumped. I swung around to see Henry's silhouette in the doorway of the barn and his dog standing next to him.

"What are you doing?"

"How did you know I was out here?"

"Mops. She was barking, trying to get out. What are you doing here?"

I told him about James, about my father, but it was when I told him about my mother that I started crying. He led me over to a bench by the door and we sat down, me talking the whole time fast and pressured and Henry just nodding. In the light from the doorway I could see he was looking at me hard, like he was trying to make sense not just of what I was saying but of all of me.

"Liza, maybe he did love you. Maybe his parents—"

"No! I just thought he loved me."

"But maybe he did. Maybe—"

"No! He never told me he loved me. I just wanted him to love me. I wanted someone to love me. Even my own parents can't love me, and you know why?"

"Liza—"

"Because I am hateful. Because no one can love such a terrible, sick, hateful girl. I will kill myself this time. I will—"

I started out of the barn but Henry grabbed my arm."Liza! Liza, look at me." He turned me toward him, his hands on my shoulders, but I just shook my head, over and over, thinking Hateful, hateful, hateful. *"Liza." With one finger he lifted my chin to look at him, a gesture so tender I stopped crying. "Liza, I am sorry about James but you are not hateful. Difficult, a puzzle, but not hateful. And* I *certainly don't hate you."*

"Does me a lot of good," I said. "You're going to college to be an engineer. Isn't that all they do, difficult puzzles?"

"Very funny. Come on. I'll drive you back to the convent. You're going to be in trouble again, Liza. Are you always in trouble like this?"

"Pretty much."

We drove back to the convent without a word but every time I glanced over at Henry he looked back at me, shaking his head, but then when he thought I wasn't looking, I caught him smiling.

He seemed suddenly older, and when we were almost home I said, "I'm glad you don't hate me, Henry Simpson. I need a friend."

"You'll always have a friend in me, Liza."

Inside, Sister Christine was sitting in the front room. She looked up from her knitting but didn't get up. "Come here, child."

I stared right at her, ready to fight.

"Go upstairs and go to sleep, and before you do I want you to pray. I want you to ask for God's help, ask for his love to help you complete this part of your journey so you can go on."

"I think God has forgotten about me, Sister Christine."

"God does not forget about his children, Liza." She must have seen the disbelief on my face. "But just in case, I will pray tonight too and ask him to check in on you a little more often now."

I nodded. I want to be worthy of Sister Christine's caring, her prayers, of somebody's love—even if it's a God I'm not sure I believe in.

Chapter 16

My arms were about to break from the thirty-five shopping bags I had in each arm. I must love doing this to myself. Every year I say I'm going to have my Christmas shopping done by December first and every year it's me and the other disorganized lunatics running around the mall on Christmas Eve, waiting in those crazy lines. And could they possibly turn down the heat? Don't they know we're all dragging around these coats? Anyway, I dropped the bags at the door and went straight to the fridge, popped open a Diet Coke and flopped onto the couch to catch my breath. It was five o'clock and I was supposed to be at Children's Hospital at six to do a holiday story time for the children on the oncology ward. Then I was meeting Scott for dinner at seven thirty at Café Venezia. I started doing the story time when I was getting my master's degree and just kept it up every year since then. I read books. We sing Christmas carols and you try not to have the whole thing break your heart. Truth be told I have to make myself do it every time. It's hard. Seeing those kids.

Wondering which ones will still be around to see next Christmas.

When I got there the kids were finishing up dinner. Two little boys, about six, were fighting over a Matchbox car. Some parents hovered around the table, helping their children eat, eating off trays from the cafeteria or talking softly in groups of two or three.

"I had it first," one of the boys yelled and a nurse stepped in, talking gently yet firmly to them.

The unit was, thankfully, not that full. One year all the beds were full and some of the kids were too sick to even be carried to the day room, so afterward I went to their beds and read them each a story.

"Hi, May," Jenny said. She's the charge nurse for the unit and has been there for years, way before I started doing the story times.

Martin, another old-timer, waved to me from the rocking chair where he was rocking a little girl who seemed to be sleeping through all the noise.

"Miss Simpson is here," Jenny called to the children. "Let's show her that we know how to sit quietly on our story blanket." She helped the kids each find a place on the blanket, negotiating a few pushes and shoves from the little ones. A little boy, no more than two, looked around frantically, spotted his mother and ran to her, where they sat on the couch together.

I started off with *The Snowman* because then you can follow up with a rousing chorus of "Frosty the Snowman." They were all in their PJs, some in Christmas PJs, some with hair, some without, some too thin, but by the time we got to *'Twas the Night Before Christmas* they were all smiling.

"Sing 'Jingle Bells'!" one little girl cried out.

We did, but one father walked out, wiping his eyes, and I felt this tug inside me and had to fight back tears myself, imagining what sadness this had stirred up for him.

Escorting me to the elevator afterward, Martin said, "Thanks so much for coming, May."

"Oh, God, this is nothing compared to what you do. I should come visit more often. Maybe I can come back for Easter or something."

"Yeah, I'll talk to Jenny and call you. We usually have the Easter

Bunny come, so maybe we can pull something together with that. Have a Merry Christmas." We hugged as the elevator door opened.

I felt guilty as I stepped into the elevator. Children's was where they transferred us not long after they fished us out of the bay, and I know I avoid the place and all it elicits. Each time I'm here I find myself looking around, seeing what might be the same, trying, as always, to see if any tiny thread of a connection to my mother lies in that place we went to so soon after her death. It makes no sense, really, but I do it anyway. It occured to me, as I pushed the elevator button, that that's how I've spent so much of my life, eyes darting around, searching for something, who knows what, that will make me remember more about my mother, like somehow that will tell me more about me. And now, in her journal, I've found it, found this reckless, immature girl and a bunch of secrets. I sit, reading page after page, until my eyes are so tired the print starts to blur, but I will my eyes open and keep reading. I'm convinced if I stop and fall asleep that when I wake up she'll be gone, disappear, again. Maybe I've known, since the first page, that I will finally have my answers, and yet they won't be any kind of answers I want, that anyone would want. And so I read on, a strange kind of pressure, pushing me to the end.

The elevator door opened and I realized then that the elevator had gone up. I wasn't standing in the lobby but on the forth floor—the psych unit. I know because over at the nurses' station I see a nurse who looks too familiar. I found myself walking up to the desk.

"Can I help you?"

"Is this still the psych unit?" I asked.

"Sure is. Forth floor, psychiatric unit. Are you looking for someone?"

"I was here once," I told her, "when I was a kid. That woman"—I pointed to the nurse I remembered—"she was here."

"Eileen? Hey, Eileen, come here a minute." Eileen put down the pen she was charting with and came up to the counter. "You remember this woman?"

"Why?"

"She was a patient here. How long ago, dear?"

"Over twenty years." Suddenly I felt so stupid. What was I doing here? How was some nurse who sees a million kids going to remember me, and who cared, anyway?

"Jesus, you're dating me now? I was ten," Eileen joked with the other one. "I was like Doogie Houser. Well, obviously it had a happy ending," she told me. "You look good and healthy now."

"Thanks," I said. I left thinking, *That's exactly what you deserve, May, you idiot.* Sometimes I'm just sick of myself. I really am.

Angry, I drove to Café Venezia, darting in and out of traffic, cursing drivers, annoyed at myself. For all the stuff I laid on Buddy about finding peace I was one to talk. Maybe what I needed was to listen to my own advice. I pulled into the parking lot and reapplied my lipstick in the rearview mirror. I felt weird about Scott, now that Buddy was back in the picture, and I didn't know quite what to do or what to say to him. Saying nothing might lead him on, and yet what could I say about something that so unsettled me. It felt like the mess I'd gotten myself into in the seventh grade. I was about halfway through the year and no one had asked me out. All—and I mean all—of the girls I was hanging with at the time were going steady with boys—meaning they ate lunch together, did a little making out at the lockers and got their parents to drive and pick them up from a movie. I was starting to feel like one freak—like you need anything in particular to make you feel like a freak in seventh grade. Anyway, I was friends with these three guys, Dale, Brent and Don, and one night, like some lunar eclipse, they all decided to ask me to go steady. I mean, we were just friends. Anyway, I was so excited I was finally getting asked out I say yes—to all of them. I'll never forget it. Dale was the last one to ask and after he left I beelined it upstairs and found Kate.

"Oh, God, Kate, you've got to help me."

"What?"

And I told her.

"You are so joking?"

"Oh, no, I'm not." I sat down on the edge of the bed, nervously pulling at a run in her bedspread. "What am I gonna do, Kate? They're all going to be at school tomorrow." I could just imagine them, like a nightmare, lined up at my locker, waiting to be made out with.

"Do you even like any of them?"

"Oh, yeah, I like them all."

"I mean, like them like a boyfriend?"

"Brent. I like Brent."

"Yeah, well, I would have thought it was him. All right, here's what you do." And like a little general, she told me how to call the other two and let them down gently. I can't remember the details now but I do remember thinking it was inspired. I felt like I could breathe again as I ran down to the den to call. So, as you can see, I hadn't made very much progress in this area except I can tell you that if I had to choose, and I think I did, I had to choose Buddy.

Scott was sitting at a table in the middle of the restaurant, over by the fountain. Café Venezia is set up to look like the inside of an Italian courtyard, with a mural of old stone houses painted on the wall, a fountain in the middle and actual laundry hanging from clotheslines that run from wall to wall. Scott had ordered a bottle of red wine and was doing the old taste test as I came up to the table.

"Thought I'd order something a little special," he said as I leaned down to kiss him, and just that, the kiss, felt suddenly wrong. "Try this. It's great."

I sat down and tried the wine the waiter poured for me.

"Wonderful." I smiled.

"I haven't been here in forever." Scott glanced up at the laundry.

"Yeah, it's great here," I said, thinking, *You are one asshole, May. This is a nice guy.*

"How did it go with the kids?"

"Fine. Hard. I mean, I'm glad I did it. I'm always glad I did it, but I always end up feeling like I haven't done nearly enough."

"Know that feeling." He took a sip of his wine. "I've had that with some of my students over the years. You can tell, by the way they show up at school, by how they act, that things are much worse than you can fix with a one-to-twenty ratio in a classroom. It's frustrating—and heartbreaking. It's good you do it, though, May. For the parents too. I bet they all could use a little normalcy."

I just nodded and we moved on to other subjects, Morgan, what to order.

When the salad came he said, "You know, I don't have Morgan for

New Year's. I was thinking maybe we could go up to Calistoga for a weekend, do the whole massage, mud bath thing, stay at a nice B and B."

And that was it. I couldn't even look at him. *I am such a jerk.*

"What? Did I say something wrong? I mean, if that feels too—"

"Oh, God, no, Scott. You didn't say anything. That's so nice of you. It's a wonderful—it's me. It's—I—" I sighed, forcing myself to look at him, and told myself I was going to at least give the guy the respect to look him in the eye and tell the truth. "Buddy is back in town. I saw him last week when I met my dad to get the tree. We talked. We had breakfast. I—I think it's possible we could get back together."

"Oh."

"Yeah. I'm sorry. I don't know. Maybe I should have said something sooner, but we haven't even really gone out on a date or anything. I just feel—"

"No, no, May. We never said we wouldn't date other people."

"Still. Look, Scott. I really like you. You're such a great guy. I just—there's this thing between me and Buddy. He was my—"

"He was your true love. I know. I can tell by the way you talk about him. I felt that way about Gail. Maybe I still do—not that it matters."

"Yeah, and I just know I have to see where this goes. There's lots of issues. I have my worries and yet—"

"May. May, really. I understand. I'm disappointed but I understand."

"You're too nice." I dropped my head in my hands. "You need to be a little pissed off or something so I can feel righteous and feel you're being unreasonable." I peered up at him and we smiled at each other.

"I do think it's your responsibility to try to fix me up with a nice friend of yours or something. I mean, it's Christmas Eve, so I'm thinking a really nice and beautiful friend."

"I'm so sorry," I said, tears welling up in my eyes.

"What are you crying about? I'm the one who just got dumped. Come on, let's have some more wine and enjoy this."

And it was a little awkward but we did. I shared a butternut squash ravioli and he shared a slice of pork roast. We talked about our week like maybe we'd do it again although both of us know we wouldn't, at least not in the same way.

I cried most of the way home, the way I do every time I let go of something, whether I want to let go or not.

"You better not be screwing up again, May," I said aloud to myself, but I knew, right or wrong, I had to go down this path, see where it took me. Finish up something, one way or the other, that's been left hanging for years.

I was lying in bed the next morning when the phone rang.

"Merry Christmas! Come on, Simpson. Get dressed. Let's go for a run."

"Hi, Buddy."

"You up for it?"

"It's Christmas morning." I groaned, looking out the window at the gray sky.

"And? You're going to be sitting around feeding your face all day. It's supposed to start raining this afternoon. You're gonna kick yourself if you don't go now."

"I have to get dressed."

"Throw on some sweats. I'll be there in ten minutes. I'll buy you a cup of coffee afterward."

"It's a deal. See you in a bit."

As I started to hang up, Buddy began yelling, "May! May!"

"What?"

"Address, sport. I need the address."

I gave him the address and padded into the kitchen for some juice and switched on the coffee maker. Dressed in sweats, a T-shirt and a sweatshirt, I pulled my hair back in a ponytail, washed my face and brushed my teeth, alternating slugs of coffee and orange juice. I was grabbing my running shoes from the bottom of the closet when the doorbell rang.

"This is nice," Buddy said. "This is perfect for, you know, a single woman, real safe and all." We both rolled right over that one, right over how it was thanks to him that I was living in the perfect-for-a-single-woman townhouse. Whatever. I could have found someone else. I just didn't.

We ran down Mecartney Drive, turned right at the water and ran the path along the rocky shore. The water was rough and brown. The air was windy, damp. I could tell it was going to pour later.

We ran for a while, hard, fast in silence. I was keeping up.

"You're out of shape, Cane."

"Nah, I'm just being nice." With that he took off ahead of me.

I raced to catch him. "Okay, okay," I called after him. He slowed down. "So what are you doing for Christmas?" I asked him.

"You know, Angela's making the lasagna. My brothers are coming, the kids. Did I tell you Jill and Chris had another baby? A boy this time. What about you?"

"I'm supposed to be at Henry and Betsy's at two. Jack's coming by."

"Scott?"

"He's with his daughter." I wasn't ready to tell Buddy I'd broken up with Scott.

We ran along for a while without talking. I looked out onto the bay. It looked just like that day my mother drove us into the bay, and the air, the wetness in the air, was the same too. I looked away.

"Christmas is easier," I said, "than Thanksgiving was. Having Kate gone. Maybe I'm just more used to it. It's been seven months now after all."

"You know she'll be back. When she's done doing whatever she's doing. When she's played out whatever it is, she'll be back."

"You're right, but I just know that something about that journal is connected to why Kate left. I just don't know why she wouldn't tell me."

"That's Kate. She does her own thing. You need to do yours."

We circled back past my street to the shopping center, got coffee and started walking home.

"Good run," Buddy said.

"Yeah." I watched him, drinking his coffee, looking in the store windows. He was so handsome, his face flushed from running, his hair messy. I felt like I did all those years ago when we first started running together, like I'd trip all over my words if I started to talk.

"I still love you, May," he said then. "You probably don't want me to say that, but I do."

I gazed right into his eyes like I was hoping to see something, but I couldn't tell you what."It's just—" I started.

"I know, May. Jeez, you think I don't know who I'm dealing with?' He put his arm around me. We walked toward home like that, sipping our coffee. "I'm thinking of applying for this spot in Fire Prevention, arson investigator, thinking maybe that might be a little more my speed."

"Like, you go out and check out the causes of fires?"

"Yeah, I mean, I don't know if I have the experience they want, if they'd train me."

"God, Buddy, you've got to check it out. Have you talked to Kevin?"

"Not yet. I'm just considering it. I thought I'd wait—"

"Wait? Don't wait. Talk to Kevin. This is perfect for you. You could be like the guy in *Young Men and Fire.*"

"Yeah. Yeah. You think so?"

"Absolutely." I stopped and faced him. "Buddy, look at me. You'd be out there again. Not just waiting at the station for the guys to come back, to hear about what *they* did."

"I know," he said slowly. "I really want this. I don't know, with my arm, if they'd—"

"I think what you need for the job is a brain—and experience with fires, and you have that."

"I'll talk to Kevin tomorrow."

"Promise?"

"Yeah. I mean, can't hurt to apply."

When we got to my front door he pulled his keys out of his pocket.

"I'm going to head out," he said. "So, you going to let me take you out on that real date? I mean, I know you and Scott are going steady and all—"

"I broke up with Scott," I said, without thinking.

"What?"

"I don't want to talk about it with you, okay, but I did and I don't feel so great about it."

"You didn't have to."

"I don't think you can say what I need to do."

"What are you getting angry with me for all of a sudden? I didn't make you break up with the guy."

"I'm not angry with you."

"You sure sound angry."

I reached into my pocket for my keys. "I'm sorry. I think I just feel guilty about it, anxious about us. Ignore me."

"It's okay. The moodiness is coming back to me now."

"I am not 'moody.'"

"Oh, yeah, that must have been some other girl I was engaged to."

"Oh, fuck you, Buddy," I said, giving him a shove, and when I did, I shoved the prosthetic arm, felt it give. "Oh, God, I'm sorry."

"It's okay, May. It doesn't hurt, you know."

I looked away, feeling stupid, but then his hand was on my face and we were kissing. When I opened my eyes he was looking at me with that crooked Buddy smile.

"What?"

"I'm just glad I came back."

"You trying to tell me I'm preferable to a boat of dead fish? That's very romantic."

Chapter 17

7/14/72

It's so hot. I sit in the church just to stay cool. I haven't written in a while because it seems to me that each day is the same as the next, except I get bigger and the weather gets hotter. It's this horrible steamy heat that leaves me all sweaty and smelly. All I want to do is go to the beach, but since I'm pregnant I couldn't go even if I knew how to get to the Jersey Shore. When I'm not in church or doing chores I convince Sister Helen to walk over to Henry's farm. Mrs. Simpson makes us lemonade and we sit in the back of the barn where it's dark and cool. Yesterday Henry filled two big metal buckets with water and we sat on a bail of hay and soaked our feet. After the lemonade the baby started to move. I talk to her sometimes now.

"Want to go swimming?" I asked her, kicking my feet in the bucket.

We all laughed and then Henry said, "How pregnant are you, Liza?"

"Dr. Price said last month I was four months so I must be close to six months now. I lose track except I know he said the baby is due in Novem-

ber."

"Henry will be gone by then," Helen said.

"Yeah, but I'll be back by Thanksgiving."

"I may be gone by Thanksgiving." Just saying the words suddenly made me so sad. As much as I missed Los Angeles and my friends, I'd grown to love all the green and Sister Christine and Sister Nancy. I was even looking forward to reading whatever Sister Mary Katherine had in store for us in September. And, of course, I would miss Helen and Henry.

"Will you stay here, Sister Helen?" I asked.

"I think so. It depends on the Mother Superior and where I'm needed. I'll go wherever I'm needed."

Henry and I smiled to each other and Helen saw us and blushed.

"Oh," he said. "Sister Helen, we're just teasing. We think you're so good to do what you're doing."

I will miss them both so. They've become my true friends.

7/21/72

Joanne is gone. I helped her pack one small bag she could carry, then kissed her good-bye. I had ten more dollars from Daddy and I gave it to her. She will be at some house in Haverford where she can have the baby and stay until she finds work. The people who run the house say they'll let her keep the baby there. The Sisters tell us that too but then no one does and so Joanne thinks they take the baby while you are still asleep from the medication. I felt so scared for her. My heart pounded so I could hardly sit still. This morning when Sister Nancy asked where she was I said I didn't know, that I thought she took an early walk. When she wasn't home by lunch I thought they knew. They don't suspect I know anything because I'm such a good liar. Today, for the first time, I felt scared to have this baby. And I felt scared to give her away. For a change when I sat in the church I really prayed. I prayed for God to take my fear.

8-4-72

Sometimes I want to call James. I know I should hate him and wish he was dead but I still love him. I don't tell anyone this. Not even Henry and

Helen. I know they would think I was stupid and for all the evidence I give people to think I'm stupid I guess I don't need to add one more thing. It's too hot. I had the window open last night and the air just sat on me like a wet towel. I felt like I couldn't breathe. I didn't take my medicine yesterday. It always makes me feel like I'm pulling myself up from this sucking place, and with the heat I knew I would just suffocate. And you know what? I feel much better. Lighter. Which is a wondrous feeling after so many days and weeks of being so big and heavy and hot. I think I will not take it today. Sister Christine gives it to me with breakfast each morning and she is not a nurse so she doesn't wait to see if I cheek it.

8-6-72

I hate myself. Helen asked me what was wrong, said I looked wild in my eyes, that she was calling Dr. Price. I told her to shut up. She gasped and I called her such a priss. That made her cry and run out of my room, and I know she went right to Sister Christine because in a minute Sister Christine was standing in my doorway.

"Liza?"

"What, you big fat cow?"

I'm sure if she was not so holy she would have slapped me but it felt so good to say. I like Sister Christine but she is fat and besides I'm angry. I'm sick of being here. And now she's locked me in my room until Dr. Price comes. I think I probably have a couple of hours until he gets here. And they are so stupid. I can climb out the window and slide down the roof in a second if I feel like it. And as soon as I'm done writing this I may feel like it. It can't be any hotter out there than it is in here.

8-29-72

I'm back. They sent me to Haverford Psychiatric Hospital. I'd been out on the roof of the convent when Dr. Price walked up the front path. I called to him and waved and all he said was, "Hi, Liza. I'll be right up."

And he did. He came up and sat on the roof, like he was used to pulling crazy girls back in through windows. Later, when he came to see me in the hospital, when I felt more myself, I remembered that and I asked him if he'd done it before.

"Yes, Liza. I'm afraid I have."

"How?"

"I had a sister with your illness."

"Had?"

"She killed herself when she was eighteen. Threw herself in front of a train at the Bryn Mawr station."

"Oh . . . I'm sorry." I truly was, especially because telling me seemed to make him so sad.

"It was very tragic—a girl dying so young. You need to take your medication, Liza. You need to stay healthy—and keep your baby healthy."

I nodded and looked at him hard.

"What, Liza? What's the matter?"

"Are you going to take the baby when I'm still asleep from the medication?"

"We would take the baby and give him or her to the couple who adopts. Haven't the Sisters told you that? Liza, as you know, I've done this a great deal and it has been my experience that if you see the baby it will be that much harder to give that baby away."

"What if I decide I don't want to give it away?"

I saw him stop, surprised, no doubt thinking what to say to me.

"It would be your choice, Liza. I'm sure you've been told that. I know some places do what you say, steal babies. But you must know the Sisters would never do such a thing. They only want what's best for you, for you to have a chance to reclaim your old life. Go on and date, and go to the movies with your girlfriends—"

"I'm going to college," I told him, and again he seemed surprised, which made me angry. "I'm smart, you know. I may behave stupidly but I have a smart brain."

"I don't doubt that," he said, smiling at me and getting up from his chair. "I'll be back to look in on you in a couple days."

"Don't tell the Sisters what I said about keeping the baby."

"I won't Liza, but you should avail yourself of their wisdom and the love they have for you. In any case, they need to know your wishes before the baby

actually comes."

"And I don't know that I want to keep the baby. I'm not saying that. I was just wondering what would happen if I did want to."

"I understand."

The Sisters called my parents, of course, when I went into the hospital. When Sister Christine came to visit she told me they were "saddened and disappointed." I told her they were just happy not to be here to deal with me. I know, by they way she looked back at me, that I was right, that she knew it too. I know they wish they had some other daughter, a daughter who wasn't crazy and a slut. Sometimes I understand, wish I wasn't so bad too. If I weren't so bad they would be able to love me. Maybe James figured it out, that I was bad, and that's why he married someone else.

Henry came to visit me the very next day after they put me in the hospital. I barely remember because they had given me so much medication. He didn't come back for another week after that when he did he sat in a chair pushed way back from the bed. He acted strange. After he left I asked the nurse if she remembered him. She laughed and said, "Oh, yes, Liza. That's the boy you tried to kiss."

"No!"

"I'm afraid so."

I threw my hands over my face. I was so embarrassed. When I saw him the next time I said, "Sorry, Henry, for trying to kiss you like that."

"That's okay. I guess there are worse things a girl could do to me."

Then he took out the big piece of marble pound cake Mrs. Simpson had sent for me and we split it. Henry's such a good friend. He came to visit me three times, just like Helen. He leaves in a week for college and I will miss him so.

9-3-72

Henry left today and it rained. Mr. Simpson drove Helen and me back to the convent while Mrs. Simpson helped Henry pack the last of his things in his suitcase. They bought him a typewriter as a going-away gift. Helen bought him a beautiful fountain pen. I bought him stationery and stamps and 5 envelopes addressed to me. He smiled and shook his head when he saw them.

"You're always doing that," I said.

"You give me every opportunity. Did you think I wouldn't write to you, you silly girl? And remember, I'll be back in November and maybe you'll still be here, and if you're not you'll be right over at Bryn Mawr College and I'll come by there to see you, unless you go home to L.A. for the break."

"I'm not going home for anything."

Father had sent me the papers from Bryn Mawr confirming my admission for the spring semester. And he'd enclosed a check for one hundred dollars and a note that they would be going to France the last two weeks of November for some business he had. He'd checked with the dean and it would be fine for me to stay there during the semester break . I didn't want to go home anyway. I don't ever want to go home. I hate them both.

9-18-72

I saw Dr. Price today. He said he is decreasing my dosage of lithium. He said he agreed with Dr. Lane that we shouldn't stop it completely but that he was hoping to be able to have less of it in my system. He made me promise I would tell him the minute I started to feel queer. I promised I would and I meant it. I don't want to go back in the hospital again and I don't want to leave here. I keep thinking I don't want to even leave here to go to college.

I got my first letter today from Henry. He likes Berkeley a lot and is sharing a room with a boy named Greg who is from L.A. He asked me if I knew him but I never knew anyone named Greg. He said they are giving him a lot of studying and he spends most nights in the library reading. He's afraid he won't pass his chemistry class but I know he will. Henry is so smart and such a hard worker.

I let Helen read the letter and she said, "I think he misses you."

"What makes you think that?"

"Oh, Liza, you know Henry is sweet on you."

"No, he is not." It had never occurred to me that Henry would like me. He just always seemed so much like a friend, perhaps more than a friend, but still.

"I think he misses us both," I said, and you could tell she liked that. I think we all feel an empty feeling after being together almost every day.

9-26-72

We are reading Hemingway now in Sister Mary Katherine's class. I think these are really boys' books. I asked Sister Mary Katherine if we could read some girls' books and she said the next one is a love story but that I needed to read The Old Man and the Sea *first. I'm trying to care whether or not he catches the fish, but I honestly don't see what all the fuss is about. It's just a fish. What is he going to do with a fish that big if he catches it anyway? Truly though, it's nice to be back in school, and the weather is cooler now. I wore a sweater to class today for the first time and this afternoon when Helen and I took our walk I could imagine the leaves starting to change colors soon. I have a new roommate, Marian, from Boston. She came with three big suitcases in a big chauffeured car. She started to have airs with me and I put her right in her place. I told her everyone was the same here—pregnant—and she could just stop thinking she was better than little Cheryl-Ann, who is clearly not from a very good family. She has bad teeth and bally sweaters and could wash a little more often. Now she hardly speaks to me but I don't care. I'm glad I said it. When I told Helen she, of course, told me I needed to remember Marian is just another of God's frightened lambs. I told her Marian made it hard to remember that.*

10-3-72

Another letter from Henry today. He got an A on his first chemistry exam and is feeling much more confident. He said he and Greg and the other boys in his house go out some nights for hamburgers and fries and milkshakes. It made me remember when I used to do that. I went right down to Sister Christine and asked if we could have hamburgers, fries and milkshakes for dinner tonight. She said she would check with Marcy. It won't be as good as the diner, but really I'm so big now I just don't want to be seen in public even if I could leave to go into town.

10-6-72

Today Sister Christine called me into her office to talk with her about the baby. She'd met with a couple this morning who were hoping to adopt a baby soon, and she thought they would be loving, stable parents for my baby. As soon as she said that I felt my throat start to close up tight and I squeezed my eyes shut to keep from crying. Finally, I got out, "I'll think about it."

"Liza, they were a lovely Catholic couple. They haven't been able to have their own baby and I think all that waiting has made them even more earnest to provide the best care possible for the baby they adopt."

I just nodded. I had seen them coming out of her office on my way back from the bathroom. She had teased blond hair and big eyes and he wore sable trousers and was much taller than her. I sighed.

"You need to decide soon, Liza. The baby is due next month."

"I don't know what to do," I told her, looking up at her.

"Then you'll need to pray to God, to Jesus, to the Holy Mother and ask their guidance. You are a young girl, Liza, with no husband to support you. The road for a single mother is a very difficult one. Some women, when their husbands die, have no choice but to walk that road. You can have other babies, later, when you are married. I know you plan to go to college in January. College is a wonderful place to meet a nice young man. No one need ever know about your mistake and your stay here."

I told her I would pray and think about it.

"Think with your head, Liza. Not with your heart."

I went right into the church but the strange thing is, when I kneeled down and tried to pray, all I could think about was her saying, "No one need ever know about your mistake and your stay here." I hadn't thought about that before, about living your whole life carrying a secret no one must ever know. It made me more scared. I sat and sat until it was dark outside and Helen slid into the pew next to me. When she saw I was crying she squeezed my hand.

"What should I do, Helen?"

And she said, of course, "Only God knows," but this time I think she is right.

Chapter 18

I was late getting over to Henry and Betsy's for Christmas dinner. By the time I looked up from the journal it was already one and I hadn't showered. Then I got halfway there and remembered their Christmas gifts so had to go back. All these years I've waited for my questions to be answered and now the answers are coming fast and furious like thick snow. I have to shake my head so I can breathe and see through it. I still haven't told Henry what I've found and that Kate had found the journal and that I'm sure it had something to do with her leaving—and something to do with where she is now. I try to imagine my mother, so young and confused and mostly, so unloved.

When I was dressing I pulled out the old T-shirt of my mother's, sat on the bed and inhaled it with my eyes closed, tried to will myself to feel her hand smoothing my hair. And I let the tears come, blotting my cheeks with a sleeve. "I'm sorry," I whispered to her. "I'm so sorry they didn't love you. We loved you. I'm sorry that wasn't enough."

And as I heard myself say the words I knew that this was what I'd wanted to say to her all along. That this was and is the real question: Why wasn't the love of her daughters and husband enough to keep her here? My mother, I feel sure, must have had the same question. Why wasn't she enough for her parents to love her? Why was she so bad—even when she tried to be good? I've always had this picture in my mind, almost like a dream, of me and Kate standing off in a mist and my mother standing, just out of our reach, where we could see her but not touch her. And in this picture Kate and I are the ones alone, trying to get to her, trying to be enough to keep her. I realize now that my mother was alone too, and that it was really the three of us lost in the mist, unable to help one another. Isn't that what Laura had tried, session after session, to make me understand? That I couldn't help either one of them. That we all had to find our own way out.

I sat in the car in front of the house and gazed at Betsy through the front window, setting the table, calling things to my dad in another room. "Merry Christmas, Kate," I said softly. "Merry Christmas, Mommy."

"Get in here, May. I'm short a sous chef," Jack called to me as I took off my coat. I hadn't even noticed his car parked in front of the house.

"You're cooking today?" I said in mock horror, leaning over to kiss him as he stirred gravy with a whisk.

"He pretty much threw me out," Betsy said. "Merry Christmas, honey. That's a pretty sweater."

Jack chuckled. "Sweater? Wait till you see the thing your father's got on."

"I take offense to that," Henry called, coming in from the garage.

"That *is* awful," I said when he appeared in the kitchen, candy canes and dancing Santas on what was clearly a synthetic knit. "How could you let him wear that?"

"His students chipped in," Betsy said.

"A dime apiece." Jack winked at me.

Betsy and Henry went into the dining room to put out the glasses. I poured myself some sparkling water and watched Jack from a kitchen chair.

"You're in a good mood today."

"I am."

"I forgot you could cook." Memories of dinners he had made us at his and Kate's old place came rushing back.

"Yeah. My chef calls in sick someone has to cook. This is ready." He took the gravy pot off the burner and then peeked into the oven. "Roast is almost ready too."

"So, why are you in such a good mood."

"I don't know. I thought I would be depressed, being Christmas and all without Kate, but I think I may be over that."

"Oh, Jack, that's good. You need to move on."

"No, no. That's not what I mean. May, I know Kate's coming back. And when she does I'll be here. I have nowhere else to go. I don't want anyone else."

"But, Jack, let's say she does come back, and I think that's still a maybe. What if she doesn't want to be with you?"

"Then I'll deal with that then."

"It's a possibility, Jack. Kate has been known to be fickle. I'm not saying she didn't love you but—"

"I'm prepared for that," he said, nodding, as if he really had thought all this through.

"And?"

"And if that happens, I will have to move on. And I will be okay."

"You sound like you really have figured this out."

"I've been working on it.

"What do you mean working on it?"

"With my therapist?"

"*You're* seeing a therapist?"

"Yeah. What did you think? You Simpson girls have the market cornered on therapy or something?"

"No. That's great, Jack. I guess I'm just surprised. Good for you."

"Yeah," he said, "it's better."

The smell of the roast filled the house, thick and strong, and Betsy had made tiny roasted fingerling potatoes and green beans, lightly sautéed in sesame butter. As we began passing the food the doorbell rang. Three of Henry's students were joining us. Betsy pulled extra plates and silver from the china cabinet and Jack brought in chairs from the kitchen. This is something I always loved about my father and Betsy, the way they opened the house on Christmas to anyone who didn't have a place to go. One year Betsy found out a girl in her class had a brother with leukemia. The family had been spending all their days at the hospital and planned to spend all Christmas day there; the little boy would probably die within a month. Henry went and picked the girl up from Children's on Christmas day and she stayed with us until the evening. Kate and I had dragged out our ratty Barbie dolls, the three of us playing on the living room floor together.

"I say we take a little break before coffee and dessert," Henry said, leaning back in his chair, patting his stomach.

"We'll have to skip dessert, Henry," the taller student said. "We're serving at the homeless shelter in a half-hour. Betsy, Jack, great meal."

Henry walked them out to the car while Jack and Betsy and I started clearing the table.

In the kitchen, Jack was rolling up his sleeves at the sink. "I've got the pots," he said.

"Leave them, Jack," Betsy said. "We'll get them later."

"No, no. You two go sit down. I do this at the restaurant. It helps me digest. Just call me Jackarella."

Back out to the living room, Betsy turned on the CD player, Bing Crosby singing "White Christmas." I sat in Henry's big chair, the one with the ottoman, kicked my shoes off and dug my heals into the soft cushion.

"When your Dad gets back in we'll convince Jackerella in there to stop washing dishes and we'll open presents. Is Buddy going to stop by?"

"I don't think so. We went for a run this morning."

Betsy smiled and nodded. "Bring him by. I'd like to see him."

The phone rang and Jack yelled, "You want me to grab that?"

"I'm up," Betsy called, walking into the kitchen. I heard her say hello followed by a long silence. "Merry Christmas, Kate."

I could feel, rather than hear, Jack stop washing pots. I froze, my eyes fixed on the doorway to the kitchen, not sure I'd actually heard right.

"Yes . . . well, we thought . . . I know, Kate. We've just been worried . . ."

When I got into the kitchen, Jack was standing by the sink facing Betsy, his wet hands dripping all over the kitchen floor, and Betsy was leaning against the wall, her back to me, listening.

All Betsy said for a while was "uh-huh, uh-huh," in a way that I knew meant Kate was trying to explain, talking fast and pressured.

"Look what I found lurking out front," Henry's voice boomed into the kitchen.

Betsy's hand went up to quiet him and she slowly turned to face us. "Kate," she mouthed. I didn't take my eyes off of her so I didn't realize it was Buddy until I felt his arm around my waist. I leaned into him, still watching Betsy. And then Betsy said, "Your father is here, and May . . . and Jack . . . . Yes . . . no, that's all. Some of your father's students were here but they've left." I could tell she was trying to act like it was no big deal that Kate had called, setting a tone for me and Henry and Jack. "Oh, and it looks like Buddy is here . . . for a bit, I think. I'll let May tell you all about that."

Henry reached for the phone.

"I'm going to hand you over to your father. It's good to hear from you, Kate."

My father took the phone.

"Let's all go in the living room," Betsy whispered, handing Jack a dishtowel.

"Come on, May." Buddy led me away from the door. "That's a good idea."

We went into the living room and sat down.

"*How* does she sound?" I asked Betsy.

"I don't know. Quieter, maybe. A little scared. I'm not sure."

"What did she say?"

"She said she was sorry, but she needed to do this, that she hoped we understood—"

"No, Kate, I don't understand!" Henry yelled. We all turned to look into the kitchen where he was pacing back and forth angrily. "That's fine. What I'm saying is that if you needed for some reason to go to New York it would have been easy enough to let us know rather then letting us worry you were dead!"

"She's going to hang up on him," I said to no one in particular.

"I *am* angry. Do you have any idea how this has affected all of us—May and Jack in particular? That's fine. I don't think I have anything else to say either . . . Yes, I'll get her." He put the phone down on the counter and I stood up from the couch. "She wants to talk to you."

I hugged him. "Good for you, Dad," I whispered into his ear. And maybe because Henry had been able to be angry I felt strangely calm. "Merry Christmas, Kate." I leaned on the counter, fingering the heap of used cloth napkins by the sink.

"If you yell at me too I'm hanging up."

Did I know my sister or what? "I'm not in a yelling mood, Kate. How are you?"

"I'm okay, I guess. I . . . I—"

"What?"

"I wanted to talk to you. I wanted to ask you something."

"Are you okay?" I asked.

She was crying softly."I am. I'm just—"

"I found the journal," I said then, without thinking.

"You did?"

"I have about ten more pages to go but pretty much I've read it."

"I left it for you. I knew you'd—I wanted, anyway, for you to read it and—May, will you come here?"

"To New York?"

"Yes, Southampton. I—"

"Why? What are you doing there, anyway? What is going on, Kate?"

"I want you to come. I have something I need to talk to you about."

"About what? Why? Why can't we talk about it now?"

"There's something I need to show you. A couple things, I guess."

I sighed. The way I often sigh with things having to do with Kate, and even as I did I knew I was getting on that plane. "You could have called me," I said. "I mean, Kate, you had to have known how hard this would be for me."

"I'm sorry, May. Maybe you'll understand someday. This is just something I had to do."

She gave me the name of the airport, Islip, and a number where she could be reached. I would call her in the morning with my flight information.

"I *am* sorry, May."

Really, I thought, what could she say at that point anyway that would make any difference? She'd have one of her entitled, lame Kate excuses ready when she finally told me and if I thought it'd be anything different I was the fool. Laura once said to me that everyone gave what they could give, and with Kate and my mom I could either accept the limits or keep disappointing myself, hoping for more.

"Really, I am so sorry to have worried you."

"I know you are, Kate." Then there was a silence. There was so much to say that it was hard to start with any one thing. "You know Jack is here. It would be good, Kate, if you talked to him. I don't know where you are with him but"—I lowered my voice—"he's crazy in love with you. He's been sick with worry, missing you. He even had to go through being a suspect in your murder, for Christ's sake, so I think you owe it to him to tell him directly that it's over."

"I don't know what to say to him."

"Just tell him you're sorry you hurt him. Tell him you hope he finds happiness with someone else, that he's a good guy. That kind of thing."

"But what if I still love him?"

"What?"

"You're still jealous of him."

"I am *not* jealous. I just can't imagine that someone would take off for all this time from someone they love, without a word."

"Oh, really. I heard Buddy is back."

I opened my mouth to tell her to drop dead and then I stopped. She was right. I finally said, "Well, are you going to talk to him or not?"

"Yeah. I'd like to."

As you can imagine, Jack practically pole-vaulted over the couch when I called him. I mean, he hadn't had *that* much therapy.

"Jack, take that up in our room so you can have some privacy," Betsy suggested, and then she said to us, "Let's have that coffee and dessert now. I could use a little chocolate."

But no one was in a real eating mood. Jack came down after about twenty minutes and it was obvious he'd been crying. I got up and gave him a big hug. Poor, poor Jack.

"Sit down," I said. "I'll get you some coffee and cake." He sat down next to Henry who reached out and squeezed his shoulder.

"She says you're going out there?" Jack said as I poured his coffee. Everyone stopped to look at me and I suddenly felt all embarrassed like I did every time I got caught letting Kate talk me into something.

"Yeah, I said I would go. I mean, I have off until after the first and all."

Henry and Betsy and Buddy all looked at me like they wished I had better judgment, but Jack said, "I'll give you a ride to the airport, if you want."

"I can bring her," Buddy said.

"Either way. Just let me know."

A while later, Buddy, Jack and I all walked out together, each of us carrying paper doggie bags Betsy had made up for us. It was starting to drizzle ever so slightly.

"When are you leaving?" Jack asked.

"I'll call in the morning, try for the day after tomorrow . . . What did she say to you?"

"She just kept apologizing, asking me to understand. And finally I just asked her point-blank, 'Should I wait for you, or what?'"

"What'd she say?"

"She said, 'I don't know.'"

I shook my head. "Oh, Jack, I'll call you tomorrow." We gave each other another hug. Then he shook Buddy's hand. "Sorry we didn't get to talk, man. I've heard a lot of good things about you."

Buddy smiled, shook Jack's hand and said he knew we'd all hook up soon. Then he and I headed off toward my car.

"Vintage Kate, huh?" Buddy said when we got to my car.

"Pretty much."

"You gonna be okay?"

"Me? Sure. I'm a seasoned pro, right? It's poor Jack I'm worried about. This stuff is wearing on him. I don't know why he doesn't just get the hell out of Dodge."

"He loves her."

"Too bad for him . . . Where you going now?" I asked.

"Back to my parents'."

"Wanna come over?" I said softly.

"Yeah?"

"Yeah."

"Come here." We kissed, the drizzle mixing with my tears, our faces tilted up to the sky, and when we stopped, my head resting on the soft fleece of his jacket, I stared out at the little speckles of stars in the black sky, wondered if heaven had a sea.

I woke to the screeching of my fire alarm and sat straight up, dazed at first, before I realized what it was. I charged down the stairs and stopped short at the last step. Buddy was standing under the hall fire alarm, fanning a newspaper, the front door wide open, and I started to laugh.

"What kind of fireman are you, anyway?" I yelled over the alarm.

"I was trying to make you some breakfast," he yelled back, and then suddenly the alarm stopped.

"Oh, yeah?"

We went into the kitchen and I peered into the pan.

"I like my bacon burnt." I picked a piece up, taking a bite.

"How about the eggs?"

I opened the fridge. "Ketchup." I held the bottle up.

For the next few minutes, we busied ourselves putting food on the table.

"You got any orange juice to wash this stuff down?" he asked, leaning into the refrigerator, finally emerging with the container.

I got us some coffee and we sat down, eating in silence. Then I said, "Thanks, this is—"

"A treat. I know. You can say it," he said, giving me that smile of his, his eyebrows raised and a sparkle in his eyes.

"What time is it?"

"Like, nine thirty. I went to the Safeway, got us a newspaper." It was then that I saw he was nervous. I got up.

"Thanks." I leaned over to hug him. He pulled me into his lap and I looked into his eyes, reached out and felt the familiar roughness of his cheeks with my fingers, "I'm starving. So, even this tastes good."

"You okay?" he asked. "I mean, with all this, with last night?"

"Yeah. I mean, unless you think you'll be disappearing again to, like, Key West or something to try out the coconut-picking business."

"Don't worry, sport. I'm not going anywhere this time."

"That's good," I said, "'cause, I'm telling you right now, you take off on me again, you better keep running, 'cause if I catch you I'll kill you, you moron."

Chapter 19

10-12-72

Each day my little baby rolls and kicks and squirms. I see her in my dreams, her eyes closed, sleeping, thinking the world she is in is the world she will be in forever. I wake so many times each night so that by sunrise I am already dressed. I usually find Marcy in the kitchen and she pours me a cup of coffee and we talk. She tells me about her six boys and how she had a daughter who died one winter of scarlet fever and how she still misses her. She brings me a plate of buttered toast or a roll to tide me over until breakfast and I whisk the eggs. I am hungry all the time. I feel like I can't eat enough, or else I get full and an hour later I'm hungry again. It's quite aggravating, actually. Marcy says that each time she was pregnant she would make loaf after loaf of bread because she would eat a loaf a day—with jam and butter for breakfast, as sandwiches for lunch, to soak up gravy at dinner. Marcy's the only one who knows my plan. I am going to Miss Latelle's boardinghouse and keeping my baby. I will find a job as a salesgirl or something in Philadelphia and I will pay Miss Latelle five dollars a week for a room, food and day care for the baby while I work. I don't dare tell Helen because I don't know if her position requires her to share everything with Sister Christine. I think she knows anyway. She knows about Miss Latelle's. When Joanne gave me the number I told Helen and she already knew about her.

Miss Latelle sounded older on the phone than Mother but not quite as old as Sister Christine. She told me that she had room for one more girl and if I brought her one week's deposit she would hold a room for me. I had to sneak out and back in the late afternoon, the time we're all free to do as we please. It's a row house, not far from here. The rooms are clean enough and at least I don't have to share a room like I do now. I have sixty dollars left from the money father gave me and I imagine he will send more soon. That should keep me until the baby is born and I can find a job. The worst, of course, was walking down the street. I saw women actually look for a ring on my finger. On the way home I took my sweet sixteen ring and put it on my left hand and turned it around so only the band showed.

I will need to tell Sister Christine soon of my plan. She is growing impatient with me—or maybe she's just worried for me. Denise Carter had her baby yesterday. Her parents are coming tomorrow to get her. Dr. Price came out from Denise's room with the baby wrapped in a white blanket and Sister Mary Katherine took it from him. The baby was gone an hour later. I didn't see the couple but I saw the car pull away as Marcy was putting dinner on the table. We all ate in silence, the weight of our futures right in front of us like that, and our shame. I remember Joanne saying how she had a friend who had gotten pregnant too but that her boyfriend had married her right away and that when she saw the girl again she acted far away, like Joanne was bad and she was good because she was married, even though they both had been the same.

10-20-72

Another letter came in the mail from Henry today. He is now treasurer for his fraternity. It seems they figured out he was good with numbers, and the old treasurer was not as good with numbers as he was with beer. I had asked in my last letter if he was dating any nice girls and he wrote back this time that he's too busy for dating. That sort of made me happy. I know if Henry finds a girl he won't be my friend anymore.

Maybe because of the letter or just because the sun was out, I decided to walk over to the Simpsons' farm, pet the sheep and cows. I felt like going alone so I didn't even ask Helen this time but, as luck would have it, when I got there Mrs. Simpson was out feeding the chickens. She saw me right away so I couldn't leave.

"Hi, Liza. What are you doing here?"

"Just wanted to visit the animals. I hope that's okay."

"That's fine. You want to help?" she said, offering me a bucket.

I love to feed the chickens, the way they squawk and rush around. When I was less big Henry would have me help Katie and Mary Beth collect the eggs. Mrs. Simpson went off to check on Katie, who I could hear around the side of the yard playing house with her dolls.

The air was crisp and even at three o'clock it was starting to feel like evening was closing in. I'm tired all the time now from lack of sleep and the weight, and winter approaching makes me even more tired.

Mrs. Simpson returned and said, "Liza, Mary Beth will be home any minute from school. Would you like to come inside and have a snack with the girls? I made some muffins and I can brew us some coffee."

I take advantage of any excuse to sit in Mrs. Simpson's kitchen and smell the warm smells, take in the pretty yellow and red flowers on her oilcloth, the way she leans down to the table to help Katie with a drawing or Mary Beth with a spelling word. Sometimes she's close enough that I can smell her powder and the mixture of coffee and the dusty yard.

Mary Beth came in as Katie and I were eating our muffins, with me helping Katie to keep her milk cup balanced and her muffin between her mouth and her plate. The muffins were blueberry, still warm in the middle. I ate three, spread with butter. Mary Beth wolfed one down in three bites with a slug of milk and asked to change into her sneakers and go outside.

"Me too!" Katie screeched, running upstairs after her.

Mrs. Simpson smiled at me and called after them, "Hats and coats both, girls. It's getting cold now."

Once they were outside, with a slam of the back door, Mrs. Simpson put our coffee cups on the table and sat across from me, taking a sip. I did the same, enjoying the quiet, imagining what it must have been like to grow up in this house, eating meals in this kitchen, playing with the animals. I recognized Mrs. Simpson's quiet, serious nature in Henry as well as his father's long, lean build and eye for the workings of things.

"So, Liza, how are you feeling these days?"

"Big!" I said with a laugh.

"Yes, I remember that. The baby is due soon, isn't it?"

"Next month."

She started to say something and must have thought better of it. She took another sip of her coffee. "Would you like another muffin?"

"Oh, no, ma'am. I've had three already."

"Oh, I remember that too—always hungry."

"I think I'm going to keep the baby," I heard myself saying.

Perhaps I told her because I wished I could tell my own mother, perhaps because of the way she smiled back at me and said, "That's fine, Liza. Babies belong with their mothers and each one, in its own way, is a blessing. You'll see."

I told her about Miss Latella's house and my plan.

She looked puzzled."Why wouldn't you stay with the nuns? They care for you so."

"I don't think I can stay with the baby. I think if I have the baby I have to leave."

"Have you spoken with Sister Christine about this?"

"Only to tell her I wasn't sure I wanted to give the baby away."

"You should talk to her. Tell her your wishes. They won't put you out."

I didn't ask her how she knew this, but later, after evening prayers, I knocked on the door to Sister Christine's room. I told her I'm keeping the baby and when she asked me why, I had to stop and think for a moment. Then I said, "Because it needs its mother," and I guess that's the truth.

"This is a tremendous responsibility and commitment, Liza. A child is not a kitten you can decide to give away if it gets too difficult." Maybe then she saw the hurt in my face. I know what everyone thinks of me, that I'm irresponsible, but her voice softened and she said, "Well, then, you should get ready. Have you ever taken care of a baby? Done any babysitting?"

I told her the truth, that I haven't cared for a baby in my life.

"We'll help you. And the good Lord provided you with the maternal in-

stincts to do what you will need to do. Still"—she got up from her chair and went to the bookshelves that line the wall—"you may want to read these." She gave me two books, one by a Dr. Spock and another by a Dr. Brazelton.

It is late now and I'm tired, but I will show Sister Christine, and everyone, that I will be a good mother and read each of these cover to cover.

10-28-72

There is a lot to know about raising babies. I've read the first chapter of Dr. Brazelton's book and feel quite reassured. He gives examples of other mothers—I guess even single mothers, although I haven't gotten to one yet, who are scared and confused. It's all very interesting. I've decided that if the baby is a girl I will name her Kate and if it is a boy I will name him Lawrence. Helen asked why I picked those names and I told her I just liked them and I can pick whatever I want, I suppose, because I am the only parent.

I saw Dr. Price yesterday and he asked me how I was doing with the lower dose of my lithium. I told him the truth, that I felt fine, I thought, but that sometimes I could feel the episodes, like a shadow, closer than before. It's the best I can explain it.

"I don't want to take any chances, so close to your due date. I think we should go back up on the dosage."

I have to say I was relieved.

11-3-72

Today Sister Christine asked if I would like to call my parents and tell them the news. I burst into tears and begged her to please not make me do that. I got so upset I even surprised myself. I told her I just couldn't bear to have them push me away one more time, that I knew they would be horrified. But she is right. They will need to know. I promised I would call them next week.

11-6-72

I called this evening when I knew both Mother and Father would be home. I think I feel a little sturdier from the increased lithium. When I asked

Mother to have Father pick up the extension, she hesitated and said, "Now what is this about, Liza?" The way she said it, as if she was so sick and tired of me, somehow gave me the strength to say my piece.

When I heard Father pick up I just said, "I'm keeping the baby." I waited a moment to see if either of them would say anything and when they didn't I kept going. "I know you don't approve, but I love this baby and I'm keeping it. I can feel in my heart that it's the right thing to do and I'm hoping you will love it too."

"Liza," Mother said then, with an intake of breath, "You are not keeping this baby. We forbid it."

And as terrified as I am of her I said, "You can't forbid anything. I'm eighteen now. It's my baby. I can do what I want." I could feel how badly she wanted to smack me.

"Liza, you are in no position to care for a child," Daddy said then.

"Daddy, the nuns have promised to help me, to let me stay here until I make other plans—"

"This is ridiculous, Liza. I will not have this!" Mother shouted.

"Why? Because you're afraid of how it will look to your friends at the club? Well, I don't care! This is my life and my baby and I'm doing this."

The phone slammed down and even as I started to cry I knew where this was going.

"Liza," I heard Father say quietly, "I cannot allow this. You are set to go to Bryn Mawr next semester."

"I'm not going . . . I can't."

"You have no money and no husband."

"You mean you're cutting me off?"

"You will not disobey me. Liza, you are my one and only little girl and headstrong as can be. Maybe I've contributed to that, allowing some of your obstinacy and impulsiveness, probably too much, because of your illness, but I am telling you now, we are your parents and being in this family means obeying us."

"Then I guess I'm not in this family anymore. And I know, Father. Don't think I don't know that you are doing this because of Mother—that she's making you choose between us. Just know I know you are choosing her."

I put the receiver gently back in the cradle and stared at it, letting my tears fall. And yet, there was something so peaceful inside of me, a kind of release, a release from trying to be and get what I cannot.

This baby swirls and kicks inside of me like a dance. I lay my hand on my stomach, see myself sliding one finger into its little fist, holding it tight.

11-22-72

It's a girl. Her name is Katherine, Kate for short. She is by far the most perfect and amazing thing I have ever seen. She was born yesterday morning. Dr. Price came right away and when he gave me the medicine I was so thankful. It hurt and for the first time I became frightened and worried I had made the wrong decision. They woke me after she was born to tell me it was a girl, and then I fell back to sleep. When I woke up I was so sick from the medicine I vomited, and once they cleaned me up Sister Christine brought me Kate, swaddled tight in a pink blanket, and let me try to nurse her. Everything is so confusing and I feel so wheezy from all the medicine they are giving me, but happy and sleepy too. The Sisters are taking such good care of me with their loving smiles and cool, comforting hands. Kate is with Sister Nancy. I will sleep now.

11-23-72

It is Thanksgiving Day. Everyone is at Mass right now and Kate and I are lying quietly in bed. She can cry loud and hard, like a very angry kitten. I can rock her or nurse her or sing to her to quiet her, and knowing that I can bring her comfort is a feeling of wholeness and joy I cannot begin to describe.

Helen stayed with me most of yesterday. We took turns holding Kate and she taught me some lullabies her mother used to sing to her. This morning Sister Christine came in and Helen and I were singing one together. She joined in and when we were done she said, "A baby is the most beautiful of God's blessings."

She is right. I hope to be able to get out of bed tomorrow.

11-25-72

Henry came to visit me yesterday. He is back in town for Thanksgiving but will be leaving on Sunday to return to Berkeley for semi-finals. He brought a big bouquet of carnations and even held Kate for a few minutes until she started to whimper. Even though it's only been a few months he looked so much older.

"It must be all that good college food," I teased.

"They try, Liza. We had a new cook start at the house last week and she's very nice, but it's just not as good as my mom's cooking. Boy, she's awful little," he said, standing up to peer into the swaddling at Kate, "but she's awful cute too."

I smiled up at him and when I looked into his face, for the first time ever, I saw something else, something other than the boy I always thought of as a kind of a big brother or cousin.

"You're hair is too long, mister," I said, teasing him again.

"You must have been talking to my father."

"I would think so!"

"Oh, Liza, you should see the way people are dressed in Berkeley. My hair is nothing. And some of these girls don't even wear"—He looked out my door to see if anyone was there—"bras."

"No!"

"It's very different, that's all I can tell you. I like it and all, but I miss it here, home and—" He stopped and looked out the window, staring out onto the grounds. His shoulders seemed broader, and I could see now that he looked older in part because he wasn't as skinny. Kate began to fuss.

"Don't turn around for a second," I said. I got out of bed, placed Kate in her cradle and put on my robe and slippers. I sat in the chair next to the cradle and began to rock her. "Okay, you can turn around."

"So, my mother said you were keeping the baby."

"I am."

"How are you going to do that? I mean, how will you survive?"

"Henry, what are you saying? You always seemed to want me to keep the baby."

"Well, yeah, but by yourself?"

"The Sisters will help me. And I've learned so much since I've been here—"

"It's just—"

"Just what, Henry?" I was suddenly angry and hurt. "I thought you of

all people would believe in me and support me. Now you sound just like my parents. And if that's how you feel you can just—"

"Liza! I'm not saying that. I—I—I care about you and I'm just worried about you." But I was crying anyway. I felt so betrayed and frightened, hearing Henry's fears.

He pulled the other chair up so he was sitting across from me, but I refused to look at him, just stared down into Kate's cradle where she was by then sleeping quietly.

"Liza," he said softly, "what I'm trying to say is that I've missed you."

I looked up at him then and when I did he took my hands in his hands.

"If anyone believes in you, Liza, it's me. I'm sorry. You misunderstood what I was saying. What I mean is—"

But before he could tell me what he meant we heard someone coming up the stairs and both of us seemed to realize how it looked, sitting so close together. Henry got back up and started putting on his jacket.

"It's time for Kate's feeding," Sister Christine said.

"If it's okay with the Sisters, maybe I can come back tomorrow, Liza."

"That would be fine, Henry. Liza should be up and about tomorrow and ready to take a little walk around the grounds if she'd like."

For the whole rest of the night I thought of Henry, the rough warmth of his hands and his dark serious eyes.

11-25-72, 10 p.m.

Today Henry came back after lunch. My hand trembles as I write this. He has asked me to marry him and come with him to California. At first when he said it I couldn't believe my ears.

"Henry, I—"

"Liza, I know you don't love me but you're fond of me and I do love you. I think you could grow to love me, in that way. I haven't been able to stop thinking of you the whole time I've been at Berkeley. All the other girls are so plain or strange—just not right for me the way you are, and I know, once I'm done with school, I can make a good living and provide well for you and Kate, and in the meantime I can work at night and we can get a small place and—"

"Henry, I—"

"If you could at least think about it."

"I don't need to think about it." I was sitting on the bench we'd sat on dozens of time, watching Henry pace back and forth in front of it. It was as if the words were pouring out of him and before I could even fully form my own thoughts I heard myself saying, "Yes."

He stopped suddenly, turned to look at me. "Yes?"

"Yes. I would love to be your wife, Henry Simpson, and Kate would be lucky to have you as her father."

As it turns out, I was the only one to be surprised.

"My goodness, Liza. Anyone could see how sweet on you he was from the start," Helen said as we bathed Kate this evening.

After dinner Sister Christine asked to see me.

"You should know, Liza, that Henry Simpson came to me the evening of Thanksgiving day to inform me of his intentions. He is a good Catholic boy of strong moral fabric. It is clearly this character and a pure and heartfelt love that has motivated him to ask for your hand. I have no doubt he will be a fine husband. Still, I would like you to reflect on why you have accepted his proposal."

"I don't know what you mean, Sister."

"Today, now, you may be feeling frightened, alone—"

"Oh, no, you and Helen—I mean, Sister Helen—and the other Sisters make me feel anything but alone."

"Liza, I am simply asking you to contemplate your motivation. We both know one day you will leave here. And I know your own family has disowned you. I hope, God would hope, that you do not accept any marriage proposal out of fear or worry that a girl in your situation is not worthy of other choices. Remember, Mary, Our Holy Mother, was an unwed mother."

"Thank you, Sister. I understand now."

"I am not saying you are making a mistake in anyone's eyes. I want you to be sure you are not making a mistake in your own heart."

I went back to my room. Helen sat in the rocking chair, in the shadows, just the light coming in from the porch and the moon, rocking Kate silently.

I told her what Sister Christine said.

"I know you will grow to love Henry in that way."

I can almost not believe what has happened. I must stop writing and go to sleep. Kate will wake in a couple hours to eat.

12-28-72

There is too much to tell to fit it all in and I am supposed to be finished packing for the morning. Kate sleeps soundly in her little cradle by the dresser. I stop packing from time to time to lean down and listen to her tiny snores. Luckily I have little to bring with me. I am leaving all my maternity clothes with the Sisters for other girls to use. Yesterday I went into town with Helen and we bought me five new dresses. None of my old dresses fit me as my breasts and hips and stomach are much larger now than they used to be. Dr. Price assured me all would return to normal in time and definitely when I stop nursing Kate.

I am scared to leave the Sisters but know I will take their teaching and guidance with me and be the best possible mother to Kate that I can. We leave for California tomorrow on a plane from the Philadelphia airport. Henry has secured an apartment for us in a small town, an island really, called Alameda. It is a short distance from school and near his new job in a place called Oakland. He will go to school during the day and work at the bakery at night. I received a letter from Father yesterday, a short note really, saying he is saddened that I have chosen this course. He ended with, "Good luck to you, Liza, my dear. You have chosen a difficult and unnecessary road." He included a check for five hundred dollars, which I know is the last I will hear from them. That's all for now. I must hurry. I will write again when I get to California.

3-12-73

I am finally writing again. I unpacked the journal and put it in my nightstand but there is no time to write. When Kate naps there is so much for me to do and when she goes to sleep at night I try to eat a bit of dinner, make Henry's lunch for the morning and fall into bed until she wakes to eat again at three. I am so tired. I am lonely too. Henry works so hard and is either at school or at work, and on the weekends I know he takes us on out-

ings when he should really be studying and then stays up late to catch up. We found me a psychiatrist and he recommends I try another medication, given I am feeling so tired and depressed. I don't know that it will work but I will try. Still, I am so in love with Kate. I curse into my pillow when she wakes me at night. Drag myself out of the bed to nurse her. And then I see her sweet innocent face and am filled with shame. Please, God, forgive me. I so want to be a good mother.

3-30-73

Cannot sleep cannot sleep cannot sleep. Henry stayed home from work and is worried about me. Am supposed to be sleeping but cannot and can hear him outside trying to feed Kate the bottle and her screaming swirling swirling so tired and Henry said to stay in bed.

4-10-73

Back from the hospital. I am so ashamed. Henry's mother had to fly out to care for Kate. I am supposed to be resting. I must sleep and get better for Kate and Henry.

Chapter 20

Henry's face darkened, thumbing through the diary, stopping here and there to read a bit and moving on, nodding, and at one point he smiled, as if she had said something to him, reminded him of some secret they had shared. "I recognize this. It was on her nightstand, but I never read it of course. It was private."

"It was in a box with some dresses—they were exactly the same in yellow, blue, green."

"Those are her uniforms from the Marlborough School. I'm sure. I do remember her talking about those." He closed the journal then, placed a hand absently on the cover. "So, you've read this?"

I nodded. "And so has Kate," I told him. "That's how I found them. They were in a box together—the dresses and the diary."

We were in a back booth at Jim's. It was between lunch and dinner, three o'clock, so the place was practically empty. Our coffee sat untouched, growing colder, with a slight white foaming top. We ordered a piece of cheesecake to share and Henry took a forkful, then a sip of the cold coffee. And I could see that my father was far off somewhere, as if this information had opened a door that had been closed to him a long time ago, as if he was making his way back through it.

I watched him for a bit and when the waitress came and offered to bring us fresh coffee, leaving with the old ones, I finally asked him, "Why didn't you tell us this?" I paused, feeling like I needed to take a breath. "I mean, Dad, we were always bugging you to tell us anything about her."

"May, this wasn't mine to tell. This was—your mother was adamant that she did not want you, particularly Kate, to know about this."

"But why?"

"Well, I think you can tell from reading this, it was a different world then and your mother didn't want Kate to know she was rejected by her real father, that your mother had questioned whether to keep her. And then there was her illness. Once we got to California, when she was away from the support of the Sisters, it got much worse. My mother flew out shortly after we got to California to take care of Kate because your mother got sick again. She was in and out of the hospital. Maybe the new doctor didn't understand how to stabilize her medication. I don't know." The words came tumbling out of him then, and the way he stared past me, into someplace he was remembering, I knew to just sit and listen. "And then when she was pregnant with you they told her she needed to go off the lithium completely, and I can't even remember how many times she was in and out of the hospital. That's when my parents moved out, to take care of you girls. That was the other thing. She was always trying to protect you girls from her illness. I cannot tell you how terrible she felt. When she was well, she would be overwhelmed with guilt for not being there for you girls, for not being a good mother, for scaring you."

"But we loved her. We forgave her every time."

"I know, honey. But that's very different from her forgiving herself."

The waitress returned with the fresh coffee and we stopped while she poured and checked the creamer to be sure we had enough milk. When she left I said, "Then how could she forgive herself for leaving us forever, for trying to kill us?"

And of course there was no good answer to this question that has swirled around us our whole life like a web, defined us, haunted us and yet pushed us forward, kept us alive, with the force of its horror.

"May," Henry said weakly, "that was her illness. Your mother adored you both. The two of you are what kept her alive all those years. You know that."

"I think there's more."

"I'm telling you everything I know." He held up his hand. "I know. I know. I've withheld this information but I made your mother a promise. It was important to her and I needed to honor that."

"I think Kate knows more," I mused, "I think that's why she wants me to come to Long Island."

"I hope for you that she does."

After he paid the bill and left the tip, Henry walked with me to my car.

"When are you leaving?"

"Early tomorrow morning. Seven fifteen flight. Buddy's going to drive me."

We hugged.

"Call me when you get there," he said, holding me tight.

"Dad? Did she grow to love you?"

"What?"

"The Sisters told her she would grow to love you? Do you think she did?"

"She said she did. At least she told me so. I think we became a team against her illness, protecting her and you girls as best we could from it. I think she knew how much I loved her."

"I think she did too," I said.

I drove toward home but then kept going past the house to the water, parked in the ferry terminal and walked along the path that hugs the bay. It was windy, but the sun was bright. I pulled on my sunglasses, hurrying along, scanning the white tips of the waves for a glimpse of her, the fluttering feet, the long legs, the tips of her fingers pushing through the cold blue sea. I went to the end of the pier and by the time I looped back the sky was turning gray and peach and pink. I thought, even though I couldn't see her, I could feel her, swimming smooth, long strokes to keep up with me, watching me, until I got in the car and pulled away.

"Just drop me at the curb," I told Buddy as we drove along Doolittle, approaching the airport. It was five a.m. and we drive through the darkness, bright circles of headlights lighting up patches of road.

"You sure?"

"Yeah, go home, try to go back to sleep."

He reached across the seat with the metal arm and drew me toward him. I leaned into his chest, feeling the warmth on my cheek, listening to the thump of his heart. Then I realized how used to the arm I was getting.

"How long did it take you to get used to it," I said without thinking.

"Used to what?"

"Your arm?"

His mouth twisted in thought. "A couple years maybe. I think it took that long to get used to operating this thing," he said, holding it up."Why? Is it bothering you?"

"It never bothered me—I mean, of course, I was upset for you. I knew how shook up you were, what it meant to you. I'm not saying I wouldn't have been just as upset. I'm just saying that for me, I loved you with two arms, one arm, and I'd love you with six arms. I was just thinking I'm getting used to the—I guess the *feel* of it."

He nodded and we squeezed each other. I was spacey with sleeplessness and closed my eyes for a few moments until I felt the car slowing down, the stopping and going, and knew we were at the airport.

"You gonna be okay?" he asked as we pulled up to the terminal.

"Sure. I just have to do this. I know there's something important Kate knows, needs to tell me, and even if I'm wrong, even if this is Kate being Kate, I need to go for myself."

Once we were in the air I pushed my seat back and buried myself in two tiny pillows and blue blanket and prayed for sleep to take me. I heard the voice in the safety movie as if it were far away and had the dream again of the little boy. In the dream I see the boots running along the pier and am so, so cold, shivering, shivering, and the boy's gaze holds me like an embrace until he starts to shimmer, turns to rain and disappears. I woke up like I always do when I dream of the boy, or my mother, or that day, feeling like my insides are reaching out, like something was wrested from me.

We must have caught a breeze or something because, even with the stopover in Chicago, we pulled into Islip Airport twenty minutes early. I watched the ground crew, the baggage carts speeding around the runways. The crew were all wearing big heavy coats, gloves, hats—hats with fake fur coming out the sides—and I knew I didn't bring a warm enough coat. I was going to freeze. I sat and waited for everyone ahead of me to get off, and some people behind too, before I even got up. We were early and Kate is always late. I pulled my bag and coat out of the overhead and started down the aisle. It was then, with the suitcase wheels making their rolling sounds, that my heart started to beat faster. Once inside the baggage claim area, I began searching for Kate. When I didn't see her I walked a few steps and then moved off to the side, peering down the wide long hall. It's a pretty small airport and wasn't all that crowded. I could see down to the end but no Kate. I sat down on an arm at the end of a row of chairs, fingered the handle of the suitcase, and when I looked up, I saw her, coming out of the ladies room. I watched her, scanning the area for me, and when she spotted me she broke into a huge smile and started almost running toward me, her coat flapping back behind her. That's when I saw, *oh, my God,* that she was pregnant. Very, very, very pregnant.

"May!" she yelled, rushing to hug me.

My mouth was suddenly frozen in shock and the feel of her round hard stomach against me was the most foreign thing I have ever felt. To have a person, who you know like yourself, be suddenly and without warning in another form—my throat tightened. When Kate pulled away and looked at me she was smiling a smile I have never seen on her before. My mind scrambled to place it, to define it, and all I could think was, *grownup.*

"You're pregnant," I finally said.

She nodded. "That was one of the things I wanted to tell you."

"But, Kate, why would you—"

"Let's go. Let's get out of here. We can talk in the car on the way back to Southampton."

I stole looks at her the whole way to the car, seeing all the differences. Her hair was longer. Her face was rounder. And the stomach jutted out in front of her like it wasn't really real, so out of proportion to the rest of her.

"This is it," she said when we reached a blue Saturn station wagon. She pressed a button on the key chain and the locks clicked open.

"Is this yours?"

"It's Helen's."

"Helen?" I climbed into the passenger seat and shut the door. "As in Sister Helen?"

"Yes," she said, starting the engine and pulling out.

"How did you find her?"

"I searched her on the Internet."

"You?"

"You think I don't listen to you. You think you're the only one who can do these things."

"I just didn't know you'd ever—"

"I hadn't but, well, you know, it was important."

The dashboard clock said five fifteen and it was already starting to get dark. We drove down a highway lined by a thick forest of trees on each side, an occasional little house in view, and Kate kept talking.

"When I found the box I could tell no one had known it was there. It was taped up and covered with dust and, you know, it was marked 'taxes,' so no one would have opened it. I had just found out I was pregnant and I can't even tell you why, May, but something told me to go down there and look around. So, one day when I knew Betsy and Dad were at work, I went down there for hours and opened every box, looked through the clothes hanging on the rack in the way back. Did you know some of Mom's dresses, one of her coats, ars back there? Anyway, so I found the box. I knew those were her uniforms because I remember looking through her yearbook and her saying how much she liked her uniforms, how she liked that they were different colors. She used to keep them folded up in a plastic zip bag on the shelf in her closet, and she took them down for me once when I asked to see them. So, I brought the whole box home and read the journal and when I got to the part about her being pregnant with me, and about the nuns, I just knew I had to find Helen, that something about finding her would help me decide what to do. And so I started looking. It took me a couple nights. I mean, I listened to you and pretty much knew what to do, but I'd get stuck. I was trying to go through the White Pages but then I just tried searching her name and an article came up in the Southampton paper talking about the retreat house. She was quoted in it. So then I got the number for the retreat house and called her." She paused then, looked over at me. "Am I making sense?"

I nodded. Slowly it was coming together for me. "You left because you were pregnant."

"Because if I was going to be somebody's mother—and at the time I hadn't made that decision—I needed to find out what I could do to clear things up in my own head with Mom, to stop fighting the world and myself, pushing up and away from everything, trying to get away from my feelings about her. And I just hoped that if I came here that maybe I could do that, and if I could do that maybe I could be this baby's mother."

Then we were both crying, tears sliding down our faces, and I reached over to hold her hand. "Oh, Kate."

She took a jagged breath. "It's okay, May. You'll see. It's okay. Just not in the way we ever thought it would be."

Then she talked about the retreat. How when she called Helen, Helen told her to come right away. And that's where she'd been, living at Glaser House, a spiritual retreat run by nuns in Southampton. She had her own room and shared a communal kitchen. She cooked and sewed and cleaned and helped out whenever a group rented the house for a retreat. She took walks on the beach. And Helen had helped her to learn to be "still" inside, to pray and to wait for answers, to be ready to be this mother-person she had committed to being.

~

We drove through a large black iron gate flanked by a tall, tall hedge on either side that ran the length of the property. The car's wheels bumped along the gravel driveway that ended at the right side of the house. It was dark by now, and the windows and porch light set the huge white clapboard house in a glow. As we got out of the car I could smell smoke and looked up to see the cloud of gray coming from one of many chimneys.

"Welcome to Glaser House, May."

I started to roll my suitcase behind me and then gave up and carried it to the front walk, a walk marked by squares of blue slate in the grassy front lawn, dotted by brown patches of dead grass and old snow.

"It snowed about three weeks ago—a lot. I guess more than they've seen in a while, and this is all that's left. It was beautiful though."

The front door was unlocked. We hung our coats on one of the many hooks lining the foyer. It was warm, with the smell of the fire and food cooking.

"Let's bring your bag up. I'm on the third floor, I'm afraid. Normally, you could have your own room, but we have a big party here this week so you're bunking with me." She led the way as I half-carried, half-dragged my suitcase up the stairs after her. "I'm not such a good sleeper these days. The baby moves around a lot now and I have to keep getting up to pee—"

"Oh, my God, Kate. You're having a baby." I finally said the words that were swirling around and around my head.

She turned and looked down the stairs at me, her mouth turned up in a wistful smile. "Yeah. I know, it's amazing."

The upstairs hall was dimly lit by a single wall sconce, and Kate opened the second door of four. The nightstand lights were on on either side of the queen-sized bed and the room was furnished with a dark wood bedframe and dresser, a small matching desk pushed up against one of the large windows. An Oriental rug in reds and browns and black covered the floor. I pushed back the heavy red drapes and looked out to the front yard. I could see over the hedges across the street and to the adjoining property to my right, whose houses were equally as huge with the same sprawling lawns.

"I guess this is a pretty ritzy area," I said.

"It is. I mean, if you go into town you see that, but here we keep it pretty basic. You'll see. Everyone's already downstairs eating so let's head down. I'm sure they saved something for us."

We went down the stairs and through the living room, and I realized that the other reason the place felt so huge was that the ceilings were so high. I was struck with a feeling of airiness and space, like the inside of me was spinning around with my hands outstretched. I could see already why Kate had made this her haven. At the other end of the living room a door led to the dining room, where I quickly counted twelve people sitting around a long table. The meal looked well underway, with serving dishes half-emptied and the clinking of utensils against plates, the comforting murmur of conversations. I could smell the wood burning in the fireplace and the rich scents of the dinner. Platters of roast chicken, rice and artichokes lay on either end of the table.

"Oh, there you are." One woman stood up and made her way toward us, a woman with a strong, ruddy complexion, pale, bright blue eyes and gray hair cropped short. "May." She took my hands in hers and squeezed them. I knew this must be Sister Helen. "It's so wonderful to finally meet you."

"May, this is Helen—Sister Helen," Kate said.

"It's so wonderful to meet you, Sister Helen."

"Helen will be fine." She smiled gently.

And suddenly I was fighting back tears.

"I know, my dear. It's a lot," she said softly.

And then without thinking I said, "Is Sister Christine here?"

"She stayed at the convent until she passed three years ago." She paused, as if remembering her, and then said, "She loved your mother. Now come. Sit down. You must be famished from your long trip."

"I am so glad you decided to come, May," Sister Helen said. The three of us were seated in a small parlor on the second floor, each of us sipping from a cup of tea, a thick chocolate chip cookie balanced on the saucer. Kate was curled up in the corner of the couch. Sister Helen was in the easy chair and I sat on the rug, my back up against the couch. "For me it is a piece of my relationship with your mother that was always left undone—not meeting you girls."

"Did you keep in touch with her?" I asked.

"We did as best we could. We wrote and sometimes we called, but you know you're mother had her hands full with you two little ones and sometimes her illness, and there were times when my work made me unavailable, especially if I was out of the country."

"Did she—did she talk about us in her letters?" Instantly I felt foolish and vulnerable at the same time. I couldn't help but ask, even though I'd wanted to appear disinterested—especially to this person I didn't know. And yet I knew from the journal that Sister Helen was as close to my mother as anyone, that here was a person who could perhaps give me some small piece of what I'd been seeking. And so when she opened a small drawer in the side table next to her and slid out an envelope, I was in some strange way almost expecting it.

"This is the letter your mother wrote me the day she died. I have shared it with Kate and now I'd like to share it with you. It is really, now that you are adults, yours."

I looked to Kate and she nodded. I stood up, took the letter and sat back down.

"Would you like to be alone, May?" Sister Helen asked softly.

"Oh, no. No, thank you." I stared for a moment at the front of the envelope, at her handwriting, ran my finger over the rough edge of the stamp. Then I turned it over and opened it.

October, 4 1983

Dear Helen,

I am writing you to say good-bye. I simply cannot do this any longer. Not any of it. I feel it happening again, that deep black hole that pulls me down and under and I know I cannot—I will not—do this again, not to myself, but more so, not to Henry and the girls. Henry sees it happening too. I see the way he looked at me this morning over his coffee cup, the way he watches me, studies me when he thinks I don't know. I see his quiet resignation, the way I know he is driving to work dreading it, yet stealing himself for what he knows is inevitable now. You know, like no one else, Helen, what a good, kind man he is. He does not deserve this life, a life where he doesn't know, from one day to the next, what will greet him when he opens that front door at the end of the day. I wish more for him. I wish better for him. I cannot be the woman he should have and I am unable to believe anymore that this will change. And I can't help but see that he is weary himself—from hoping for something that never happens each time we cycle through this ordeal. He does not know it now, is too good to admit it, but he will be relieved. And then there are the girls. They are, as you know, my reason for living. I love them more than air. This morning, after cleaning up the breakfast dishes, I walked toward their room where they were playing and I could hear them. They were yelling, "The bad eyes! The bad eyes! Hurry! Hurry, hide!" Then they ran into their closet and slammed the door. This is their life, Helen, a life where they must try to make sense of what no child should have to experience. Don't you see? They believe some facet of their mother is a monster they can hide from in a closet. But, of course, it is much worse because they come out to get dressed and here I am. And even little May watches me, knows what is happening. I can see the fear in their little faces and yet a tiny courage that tears at my heart, and it is only me that can put a stop to it. What I struggle with now is what it would mean for them to be motherless—even with having had a mother as lacking as myself. I cannot imagine heaping yet another burden on their little souls. And so, I think perhaps I will take them with me, that perhaps the love of God and the eternal joys of Heaven will bring peace finally to the three of us—but I am not sure. I have prayed all morning for clarity but no answer has been forthcoming. I had hoped in writing to you I would feel closer to God and an answer. Helen, thank you for your friendship all these years and for your kind and gentle guidance. Please know that I will always love you. Please pray for Henry and the girls. If you are right, and you always are, that God opens his arms to all sinners, I will see you in Heaven. I know this will cause you pain and I am sorry. Please know this is the only thing I know to do to stop my own suffering and hurting those I love. I wish there was another way.

Love, Liza

I stared at the letter long after I finished reading the words.

"Thank you," I said finally.

"It is not, I'm sure, the comfort you had hoped for."

"Yes," I said, looking up now at Sister Helen and Kate, "but it's the truth."

"There is one more thing that you need to know. There was another baby, stillborn, when Kate was born. He had died early on in her pregnancy and was maybe only a pound. The decision was made by the Sister Christine and Dr. Price to have the baby baptized, bury him in the convent cemetery and to not tell your mother. It was thought she was too fragile to handle such news. I didn't agree at the time, but I was in no position to oppose them and later, with all the turmoil she was in—well, it wasn't something you shared in a phone call anyway. He was baptized Lawrence Joseph Small. I wanted you to both know that you had a brother, that you have another angel in heaven watching over you."

A while later, after we'd finished our tea, I decided to take a walk. Sister Helen gave me the code for the gate and once outside the gate I turned right and kept waking down the sidewalk, which was lit by street lamps. It was quiet and the sound of my shoes hitting the cement made a small echoing sound. I shoved my hands in my pockets and hugged my coat tight around me, my right hand still holding the letter.

My mind was swirling with the bits and pieces of the puzzle, all the answers I had sought, answers I hadn't even known were there. How her telling us to go for the hot chocolate was her way of seeing whether God wanted her to take us with her. How in a way our Bad Eyes game pushed her to kill herself, and yet she killed herself to save us. However marred her thinking, she *was* thinking of us, doing the only thing she felt was in her power to do. And was she wrong? I wondered. Was it better to have a dead mother or a mother who was taken away time and again by her illness? Who could say? And then the boy, our brother, the son she never knew. At the end of the block, I crossed the street and kept walking. There were no people, no cars, just me and the cold air I gulped in.

As I walked the empty streets of Southampton that night I was filled with resolution—and a kind of peace—but my peace felt much more like a good-bye. "I understand at least," I whispered to her. "I understand this was your love. And despite whatever else hurts, that makes all the difference."

I could smell the ocean before I heard it, before I felt the sand between my shoes and the pavement. The road ended at a huge beach house, almost all windows, that lit a patchwork path in the sand for me. I climbed the bank of sand, up and over the dune, and there at the top I saw the Atlantic Ocean, black with white crests of waves that rolled up onto the sand with small crashing sounds. I don't know how long I stood there. A while. Even though I didn't see her, didn't quite even feel her, I said the rest anyway—that maybe it was meant to be, our going into the bay with her. How the going in, the swimming up and out, defined us forever as the survivors we needed to be—those poor motherless girls *who made it.*

Chapter 21

"All I'm saying is that when you pick a name like Lawrence you have to expect people are going to call him Larry," I said, patting Audrey a little harder, listening for the tiny burp.

"I know. I'm just saying that if you *ask* someone not to, it's just rude."

Kate ran her hand tenderly through his thick brown hair. He looked up at her from the floor where he was dissembling a Duplo structure.

"Larry!" he chirped in his sweet two-year-old's voice.

"Lawrence," she said, smiling.

Earlier he had spotted Audrey in what had once been his infant seat and decided to do away with the little interloper once and for all, taking hold of the seat and flipping it over in one quick push. Audrey, red-faced and screaming, was angry but fine.

Jack, of course, hadn't been able to get Kate home fast enough from Southampton. I figured as much. When I came back from the ocean that night Kate was still up, sitting in bed waiting for me.

"I was starting to worry," she said.

"That's a switch."

She motioned for me to come sit on the bed with her and I kicked off my shoes and climbed up.

"Are you okay?"

I nodded. Then I thought for a moment and added, "You did real well, Kate. Thanks."

She practically beamed at me. "Thanks."

We stayed up late and talked, about our mother, about ourselves.

Finally she said, "I think I'm ready to go home now."

"I think you should call Jack. You need to tell him."

"I don't want him to feel obligated, May. I'm ready to do this—"

"Are you crazy? He's going to flip when he hears this. You *and* a baby? You won't be able to keep him away."

Jack had a couple houses for her to choose from by the time we landed at Oakland Airport. She picked Bay Farm Island so she could be close to me. The baby was born in February. That spring I would rush home from work at the library and go straight to their house, sweep Lawrence out of her arms, or his cradle or infant seat, and rock and smell him while Kate ran for the bedroom and dove into the bed. Sometimes I stayed until Jack got home from his job as manager at the new swanky (for Alameda) restaurant. Sometimes Buddy came over, carrying a heat-and-serve Papa Murphy's pizza and a six-pack. Jack would say, "My God, Kate, have one. Didn't that woman in the Safeway tell you it was good for your milk production."

"She was a *drunk*! It was eight thirty in the morning and she smelled like tequila."

Kate is like one of those reformed smokers—walking the straight and narrow, to everyone else's detriment. When Lawrence was about eight months old I walked in and she had some green stuff going 'round in the Cuisanart.

"What the hell is that?"

"Organic broccoli and tofu."

"Nice color."

"It's not bad," she says, offering me a spoonful. It actually wasn't so bad—kind of creamy and tangy. Lawrence loved the stuff and Kate became Mama Puree. She had all these ice cube trays filled with colored cubes of purple beet puree, orange sweet potato puree, some rice-chicken combo that never really went over. Even now she's a little over the top if you ask me. I sneak him the Goldfish crackers and Popsicles at my house. As his godmother and aunt I see it as my responsibility to make sure the poor kid doesn't end up some freak with a pathetic yogurt-wheat-germ parfait in his lunchbox in elementary school. Jack is just as bad—running hither and yon, searching out the best farmers' markets and running out to Berkeley on his lunch hour for some organic whole-wheat tortillas Kate can't find on the island.

"Wait and see," she tells me. "Audrey's still on breast milk now."

I think not. I think if I ever get any extra time again I'm sleeping, and if that means she's eating a slab of Velveeta on a Ritz, so be it.

I still worry about Kate. There've been a few times when she started to struggle, but her doctors are right there and even during the worst period, when Lawrence was two months old, I could feel her willing herself out of it. She lost that one, spent a couple days in the hospital. It's the big picture that counts, Dr. Medley tells her, but I know it scares her. Not being stronger.

We were driving home from Lawrence's first birthday party when Buddy proposed. I could not even believe it.

"You're proposing to me while you're *driving*?"

"Jesus, May, it's not like I haven't done this fourteen times before. Give me a break. We've been living together for over a year. Don't you want to get married?"

"You are just not good at this."

"What? Proposing? So is your plan that I just keep doing it over and over until I get it right—or I die?"

We pulled into the garage and he turned the engine off.

"May," he said, turning in the seat to face me, taking my hand, "please marry me and give me the chance to love you forever."

"That's very good," I told him. "I accept."

And maybe because we were getting married, Kate and Jack decided they finally would too, so we had this little thing over at the house for them about a month before Buddy and I got married. When I found out I was pregnant a month after the wedding, I called Buddy in tears at the station. He got the Arson Investigator job and it was Kevin who answered the phone.

"You okay, kid? You need me to come over there?"

And he was so nice I started crying harder and said, "No, but I'm *pregnant.*"

"Pregnant? That's great, May."

Buddy was out on a call, so by the time he got back the whole station knew.

"You're *what*?"

"I don't think I'm ready," I said to him.

"You? Miss I-think-I-want-five?"

"That was a long time ago," I cried into the receiver.

"Chill, May, you've got nine months to get used to it." But he was home in five minutes, hugging me, kissing me, telling me what a great, though ever-so-slightly controlling mother I would be.

Even now I worry sometimes about what I really do have to give to Audrey, how I can possibly give what I barely remember. And then little things happen—a song I suddenly remember, this warm shimmery peace I feel in the quiet that takes over her room just as she falls asleep in my arms—that lets me believe each day or hour that I can do this.

I'm starting back to work in a month and just thinking about it sometimes makes me burst into tears. I cry all the time these days—happy, sad, I'm a real waterworks show. I went back to see Laura again this week to ready myself for work and of course she said this is really me doing all my good-byes again.

"I don't think so," I said. "I've done my good-byes to my mother. I think this is hormones."

She didn't doubt that, and furthermore, she explained, leaving the baby to return to work is typically difficult. Still, she would be doing me a disservice if she didn't point out that my new status of "mother" would easily lend itself to my working through my relationship with my own mother on a new level. And how could I argue with that?

"Okay," I said, "fine."

So she gave me homework.

I looked at her like she had to be crazy. "Sleep," I told her. "If I have time, I sleep. I do not have time for homework."

"I'm sure you'll work that out," she said. "I'll see you next week."

And Buddy was, of course, no help.

"I can put her down tonight. Pump me a bottle and I'm on duty."

Fine.

My assignment was to write a letter to my mother telling her how I miss her now that I am a mother. I made a cup of fenugreek tea and putzed around sorting laundry before I finally forced myself to sit on the bed and write. And I sat and I sat and then I called Kate. When I told her the assignment she said, "That's a great idea."

"Well, then, why don't you do it?"

"I did."

Fine.

I got back up off the bed and rooted around in my underwear drawer until I found the T-shirt. I sat on the edge of the bed holding it and then I remembered something. It was summer and we were sitting in my blue plastic wading pool, the water up to our middles, making my Barbie dolls swim. Kate must have been at school because it was just the two of us.

"If I could be anything in the world," I told her, "I would be a fairy princess."

"Oh," she said with a laugh, "didn't I tell you? You *are* a fairy princess."

"I am?"

"How could that have slipped my mind? Well, yes, you are the Princess of the Deep Blue Sea, ruler of all the sea creatures, and mermaids too."

"Do I have crown?"

"Of course. Where did I put that? We'll have to look for it."

And when we couldn't find it she offered to make me one out of glitter and construction paper and macaroni. As we were sitting at the kitchen table, squeezing the glue and tapping the glitter, I asked, "If *you* could be anything in the world, what would you be?"

"Your mother."

I stopped tapping my glitter then and looked up into her eyes. She swooped down, kissed me ever so softly on the neck, and then we finished my crown.

And I started to write.

About the Author

Michelene Esposito lives in Northern California with her husband, Rafael, and son, Benjamin. Her first Novel, *Night Diving*, was published by Spinster's Ink and received the ForeWord magazine's Silver Award for Gay and Lesbian Fiction. She has completed a third novel, *Storm,* and has published short stories in *Young Miss* and *Teen* magazines.

Publications from Spinsters Ink

P.O. Box 242
Midway, Florida 32343
Phone: 800-301-6860
www.spinstersink.com

NIGHT DIVING by Michelene Esposito. *Night Diving* is both a young woman's coming-out story and a 30-something coming-of-age journey that proves you can go home again.
ISBN 978-1-883523-52-7 $14.95

FURTHEST FROM THE GATE by Ann Roberts. *Furthest from the Gate* is a humorous chronicle of a woman's coming of age, her complicated relationship with her mother, and the responsibilities to family that last a lifetime. ISBN 978-1-883523-81-7 $14.95

EYES OF GRAY by Dani O'Connor. Grayson Thomas was the typical college senior with typical friends, a typical job and typical insecurities about her future. One Sunday morning, Gray's life became a little less typical, she saw a man clad in black, and started doubting her own sanity. ISBN 978-1-883523-82-4 $14.95

ORDINARY FURIES by Linda Morgenstein. Tired of hiding, exhausted by her grief after her husband's death, Alexis Pope plunges into the refreshingly frantic world of restaurant resort cooking and dining in the funky chic town of Guerneville, California.
ISBN 978-1-883523-83-1 $14.95

A POEM FOR WHAT'S HER NAME by Dani O'Connor. Professor Dani O'Connor had pretty much resigned herself to the fact that there was no such thing as a complete woman. Then out of nowhere, along comes a woman who blows Dani's theory right out of the water.
ISBN 1-883523-78-8 $14.95

WOMEN'S STUDIES by Julia Watts. With humor and heart, *Women's Studies* follows one school year in the lives of these three young women and shows that in college, one's extracurricular activities are often much more educational than what goes on in the classroom.
ISBN 1-883523-75-3 $14.95

THE SECRET KEEPING by Francine Saint Marie. *The Secret Keeping* is a high stakes, girl-gets-girl romance, where the moral of the story is that money can buy you love if it's invested wisely.
ISBN 1-883523-77-X $14.95

DISORDERLY ATTACHMENTS by Jennifer L. Jordan. Fifth Kristin Ashe Mystery. Kris investigates whether a mansion someone wants to convert into condos is haunted. ISBN 1-883523-74-5 $14.95

VERA'S STILL POINT by Ruth Perkinson. Vera is reminded of exactly what it is that she has been missing in life.
ISBN 1-883523-73-7 $14.95

OUTRAGEOUS by Sheila Ortiz-Taylor. Arden Benbow, a motorcycle riding, lesbian Latina poet from LA is hired to teach poetry in a small liberal arts college in northwest Florida. ISBN 1-883523-72-9 $14.95

UNBREAKABLE by Blayne Cooper. The bonds of love and friendship can be as strong as steel. But are they unbreakable?
ISBN 1-883523-76-1 $14.95

ALL BETS OFF by Jaime Clevenger. Bette Lawrence is about to find out how hard life can be for someone of low society standing in the 1900s. ISBN 1-883523-71-0 $14.95

UNBEARABLE LOSSES by Jennifer L. Jordan. Fourth in the Kristin Ashe Mystery series. Two elderly sisters have hired Kris to discover who is pilfering from their award-winning holiday display.
ISBN 1-883523-68-0 $14.95